NEWTON'S CROSSING SERIES
BOOK 3
A ROMANCE

A SNOWY AND SPICY Season

JEAN-PAUL PARE'

A Snowy
And
Spicy
Season

JEAN-PAUL PARE

A Romance
By Jean-Paul Pare'
Newton's Grove Series Book 3

Dedication

This one's for the neighbors in 1976. You know who you are. Thanks for the best Christmas memory of our lives.

And for all of you who like those cheesy Hallmark Christmas movies. This one's a little more spicy than those, but I think you'll like it anyway.

For M.

Acknowledgments

As always, my first reader Alexis. My best friend. Keep up the great work.

Suzette Pare', my unfailing editor. Always making my drivel better.

Cover Design by Olivia @oliviaprodesign on Fiverr

. . ❧ . .

"Jacob Marley was dead, to begin with."
—A Christmas Carol, Charles Dickens

Chapter 1

Maggie Thorne

"**H**ome is where, if you show up needing help, they have to take you in," she reminded herself, getting out of her red Honda. She'd driven across the country, from Los Angeles to Newton's Crossing, hoping she would be welcome at her father's house. Ten days ago, she'd lost her job when the Art Gallery had shut down.

She didn't blame Gerta, the owner, for having to close the store. She'd just gone over budget on advertising a new and upcoming artist, only to have the show be a bust. Who knew surreal paintings and sculptures of cats cavorting with dogs and ducks wouldn't hit the highbrow needs of the California art loving community?

Gerta sold seven of the twenty-five pieces, and she had to lower the prices to even do that. It was a make-or-break show, and boy did it break. So, Gerta Lundgren had shut down the gallery for an indeterminate amount of time. She still had a large selection of art from other shows, and would contact Maggie when she reopened.

"I'll call when things get back together," the young blonde woman had said, tears in her eyes. Maggie and two others who had worked for Gerta for the past fifteen years were let go. She was able to pay Maggie her last paycheck, close to two thousand dollars.

Maggie had decided to take a few months off to see what the next phase of her life looked like. And that started in her hometown, Newton's Crossing, North Carolina. She had tried to call her father a few times, and had left voicemails, but they weren't returned. She'd thought it odd, since they had talked a few times a year for the past twenty years. She knew he was a busy lawyer, but not having a few minutes in the last five days to call his own daughter back? That was odd.

It took her five days to drive across the country, using her limited funds on gas, snacks, and shitty roadside motels. But she'd made it, finally.

The noon August warmth comforted her as she walked up the steps to the large three-story white house on Banbury Hill, the home in which she'd grown up. A bed of red roses had been planted in the front yard, recently manicured. That must be Veronica's doing, her new stepmother. I just wish it wasn't sprinkling; she thought. Having the sun out would make this a bit easier to do.

The perfect green lawn showed lines of having been recently cut. She surmised it had been yesterday, since most landscapers her father hired didn't work on Saturday. The front door, painted a rich Talbot's Red, beckoned. She looked up at the third-floor windows and focused on the last one on the right, her bedroom. She couldn't wait to get there, sleep, eat in her childhood bed, see her dad and call friends she'd barely seen since she left town close to two decades ago.

She went to the door, turned the knob, and it was locked. There was a Ring doorbell next to the door, and she hit the button. A blue ring lit up and a dinging sound came from the panel. She waited.

She heard voices, a woman and a distinct, low male voice.

"Who's at the door?" said the man. This had to be her father. There couldn't be a new owner. This would be awkward if there was. Her father had never evinced a notion that he would move. Banbury Hill House had been his for over fifty years. She didn't think he would have sold it, not unless he and Veronica decided to start fresh in a new home. But her father would have told her, wouldn't he?

"I'm expecting a package from the Prairie Ladies," she heard the woman's voice say. The door knob turned, there was a click of the deadbolt snapping back, and the door opened. "Hey, just bring it in." The woman stopped dead, a look of surprise on her face.

Maggie waved, "Hi!" she said in as cheery a voice as she could. Veronica looked her up and down. Maggie heard someone come up behind Veronica and saw her father step beside her.

"Honey," he said cheerily. "You're home. Good!" He went to hug her and Veronica put her arm out in front of him, stopping him in his tracks.

"What," she said, ice in every clipped syllable. "Are you doing here?"

Maggie paused. She shook her head. "What?"

"You heard me." Veronica was wearing a white blouse and a brown muslin skirt that came down to her ankles. She stood in simple white sandals. Her hair was formed into a bun tighter than any salon worker would make it, seeming stronger than steel in how it had been erected on her head.

"I heard you," Maggie stepped closer to her father, who had averted his eyes from his daughter. "But I don't understand." She went to hug him. Veronica stepped in front of him. If this woman were a football linebacker, Maggie would have been sacked.

"You're not welcome here," Veronica spat. "I think you can understand that!"

Maggie looked at her for a long time, then back at her father, who had gone a shade of red. He didn't say anything. Why would he let her talk to her own daughter like this?

"No, I don't understand that. I lived in this home for 18 years." Maggie put her hands on her hips. This woman was about to get a throat punch. "So why don't you let me into my own home?"

"This is no longer your home, little girl."

"I'm thirty-eight, I'm hardly a little girl."

"Dressed like that?" Veronica pointed a long index finger at Maggie's clothes. She looked down. She wore a black crochet bare midriff halter top and a lace black skirt that flowed in the midafternoon breeze. Her blonde hair came down in curls on her back and shoulders. She'd dyed it with streaks of blue highlights.

"Dressed like what?" Maggie asked. "This?"

"Exactly," Veronica moved to shut the door. "Now leave."

"No!" Maggie advanced on her stepmother. "Dad, are you going to let her talk to me like this?"

"Honey," he began. Veronica cut him off.

"I don't think I'd want anybody here that looks like…" she waved a chastising finger up and down at Maggie. "…whatever this is. If you were a good girl, you would understand what I'm talking about."

Maggie vacillated between anger and hurt, and anger was winning. She wanted to murder this woman who had recently married her dad and had wormed her way into her father's heart and pants.

Her father shook his head abruptly and said, "Darling, I think you should go now."

"But where am I going to go?"

"I'm sure you're smart enough to figure that out," Veronica stepped back into the foyer, as if wanting to get away from a plague victim. "You're intelligent, I'm assuming you have your own money and can find a place to stay." She pointed to the red Honda in the driveway that had seen a lot of miles. "If not, I'm sure, whatever that is, is comfortable. Looks like maybe you've had to sleep in it more than a few times."

"That's it!" Maggie stepped into the foyer; eyes fixed on the woman who had clearly hoodwinked her father into marriage.

Veronica retreated, her arms up. Maggie's father stopped her with his arms around her waist. "I'm not going to take being talked to like this!"

"Darling," he said softly. She calmed down and gave Veronica a look that would turn the woman to ash.

"All I was asking was to stay for a few weeks 'til I found something."

"This house is off limits to you, especially when you're looking the way you look. We don't live like that here. And we expect the people who live here to not look like that." She advanced on Maggie, shaking her finger in her face. "So, if you don't mind, get off of our property!" She huffed and walked away, sandals slipping against the hardwood floor of the living room and out of sight.

"Daddy," she gave a simpering plea.

"I'm sorry, darling," he said, blinking a couple of times. "Veronica has spoken."

Maggie stepped back from her father in disbelief. She stood on the top step to her home and watched, perplexed by this exchange, as her father closed the door.

"What the fuck was that?" She shook her head in disbelief. This was a man who has stood up to the highest judges, the most powerful politicians, and even more dangerous criminals, and here he was, yielding like melting butter for this woman.

She turned around, still shocked by this exchange, went to the Honda, and sat, staring down the all too familiar road of the neighborhood where she was raised. "What the actual fuck?"

Chapter 2

Daniel Phillips

It was a dreary November morning, and Daniel was feeling morose. Today was the fifth anniversary of his wife Cassandra's death, and he knew he should go to the cemetery. But the steady drizzle outside only added to his reluctance. He could still hear the final tone of her death, the machines clicking off, the unmistakable aura of loss hanging in the air.

Why does it have to be raining? he wondered, staring out the window. Can't it be sunny just once on the day I have to go to the cemetery? He considered waiting until tomorrow—what difference would a day make? But that thought vanished as soon as he saw Bill pulling on his black Guns N' Roses hoodie.

"Ready to go?" Bill asked, not giving him a chance to put it off.

Daniel sighed, running a hand through his hair. "I really don't want to. Let's go tomorrow."

"Nope," Bill said firmly, shaking his head. "We go today."

"I should just go alone," Daniel muttered, half hoping Bill would let him off the hook. "You don't have to come if you don't want to."

Bill crossed his arms. "Daniel."

"I don't want to hear it," Daniel snapped, the frustration boiling over. "It's bad enough you show up here every day like some watchdog, checking up on me. And now I have to listen to you demand I go sit at a gravestone and talk to my dead wife?"

Bill's expression softened, but his voice stayed firm. "We do it every year. Get your coat."

Daniel sighed again, knowing Bill was right. This was their ritual. Cassandra wasn't just part of Daniel's life—she had been a part of Bill's, too. The three of them had been inseparable, like three peas in a pod. Bill and Cassandra had been close friends, purely platonic, but their bond was undeniable.

As Daniel grabbed his jacket, Bill eyed the unfinished chess game that was a constant in the bookstore and asked, "When are you going to stop letting me beat you in chess?"

Daniel snorted. "I don't let you beat me."

"Yes, you do, Mr. High School Chess Champion," Bill said with a grin.

"I'm just a bit rusty," Daniel said, shaking his head.

"Bullshit."

"I'm serious," Daniel protested weakly.

"Uh-huh." Bill gave him a knowing look. "And when are you going to tell Charlotte across the street that you've been sending her roses?"

Bill's face flushed slightly, but he shrugged it off. "Mind your own business."

Daniel smirked. "You're always in mine, every day, I might add. Why can't I get into yours?"

"Because it's mine," Bill said, his tone light but determined. "I'm trying to go the slow courtship route. Being romantic."

Daniel raised an eyebrow. "Sending her half a dozen roses every week for the last few months?"

"Three months, to be exact," Bill said, standing a little taller. "Ever since she started at La Perk."

"So why not tell her?" Daniel asked, crossing his arms.

Bill sighed, rubbing the back of his neck. "Have you seen me recently? Receding hairline, heavier than I should be?"

"You've got your sense of humor. Personality goes a long way," Daniel pointed out.

"You've seen her," Bill countered. "I'd need a whole lot of personality to get someone like that."

Daniel chuckled. "She's pretty, sure. Do you even know if she's single?"

"She is," Bill admitted. "But that doesn't matter. She's got a certain style and grace. I've got to approach this slowly."

"I bet if you asked her out, she'd say yes."

"Can we not talk about my love life right now? We've got other things to do."

Daniel's smile faded, the weight of the day returning. He glanced out the window, his eyes distant, as the rain continued to fall. His chest tightened, and a tear slipped from the corner of his eye. He quickly wiped it away. "We have to get going."

He moved toward the door, but hesitated, his hand hovering over the handle. He didn't want to open it. He didn't want to face what was waiting for him at the cemetery. Every year, the same ritual. Every year, the same pain.

Bill watched him for a moment, then walked over and wrapped him in a hug, strong and sincere. "Hey, I miss her too. Everyone does. I know today's hard for you—it's hard for me too. You're my best friend, Daniel. Always have been. And I'm not going to let you down. But if you think I'm going to let you do this alone, you're crazy."

Daniel swallowed hard; his throat tight. He didn't trust himself to speak, so he just nodded.

Bill's voice softened, but there was steel in it. "Cassie told me to keep an eye on you after she was gone. So, I'm doing it. Now get your fucking coat, and let's do this."

Daniel took a deep breath and nodded again, finally grabbing his coat. "Okay," he said quietly. He turned the closed sign on the door and locked it behind him.

"I know you're right," Daniel added, his voice barely audible.

"I know I'm right," Bill replied, walking out into the drizzle and opening the driver's side door of Daniel's Acura for him.

Daniel paused, then gave Bill a playful punch on the shoulder. "Thanks, buddy."

Bill grunted as he climbed into the passenger seat, adjusting the chair with a loud sigh. "Seat's too far forward," he grumbled. "You been driving Rose around again?"

"Yeah," Daniel said, starting the car. "Her car was in the shop."

"Is she going to be at the cemetery today?" Bill asked.

Daniel shook his head. "No. She goes when she feels like it. They had a different relationship. You hear about mothers and daughters at each other's throats, but those two were best friends right up until the end. They never argued, not once."

Bill nodded. "That's good, though. Right?"

"The best," Daniel replied, his voice heavy with emotion.

The Acura hummed to life, and Daniel pulled out onto the street. He didn't want to do this. But he knew he had to.

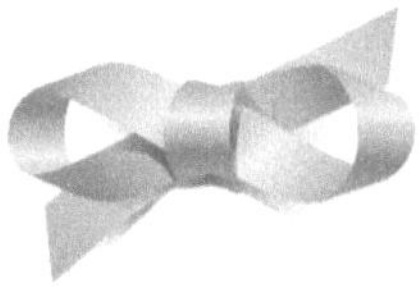

Chapter 3

Maggie

"Fucking bitch," Maggie said. "Now what am I going to do?"

She sat in her orange Honda, trying to come up with some sort of plan. She had grown up in this town; surely, she could do something. She knew people. But who could she call without being a bother? That was the question. Sure, she could call all kinds of friends, but, with the exception of a quick trip in August for her dad's wedding, it had been twenty years since she was last here. Would anyone remember her? Let alone help her?

There was Rose, but that ship sailed a long time ago when she married the Air Force firefighter and had two kids. Rose wouldn't be down for some itinerant vagabond crashing on her couch for three months. Even though Maggie could pay her, it still wouldn't be a good idea for either of them. She could stop by, but that was better saved for another day.

Who's next?

She scrolled through her phone contacts. Why was it so hard to find actual reliable friends in a small town? It couldn't be because of how she mistreated some of them, right? Spoiled little rich girl, smarter than the average bear, and wasn't afraid to let everyone know. Okay, so she burned some bridges, but that was two decades ago. Surely, no one would still hold a grudge.

She looked up at her old house again. Maybe she could just buy a prairie dress, some sandals, put her hair up in a bow, and dye it black. Take her makeup off for a few months and—What the fuck am

I thinking? She had seen the look in her dad's eyes. There was no going back there, or changing who she was to please her dad's new wife. No, fuck that.

How about Henry Connors? He had a crush on her once. Maybe she could call him. She opened Facebook and searched his profile. Oh, still a writer. With a wife, three kids, and two dogs. That's a no.

Jenny Mulwray? Let's see. Married. Farmer's wife. Happy, with a kid and two cats. Fuck.

Then she came to Kayle Harding. Her new stepbrother. Veronica's firstborn. They didn't know each other very well, having just met at the wedding, but they seemed to connect over their shared opinion of his mom. Of course, why hadn't she thought of him first? She looked at his profile. Single. Check. Living in town. Check. He had a spare room with a bed. Checkarooni. Jackpot. She found his number in her contacts. Thank God for cell phones that kept contacts from one upgrade to the next. Does he still have the same number? she wondered as she hit send.

One ring, then two. "Hello?" It was him. Thank God.

"Kayle, hey, it's me, Maggie. How you doing?" she said, trying to sound as cheerful as possible, despite the shitty conversation with her dad and stepmom a few minutes ago.

"Mags!" He sounded genuinely happy to hear from her. "What are you up to, girl?"

"I'm in town. I decided to stop by my Dad's house, and it didn't go well. How are you doing?"

"Right as rain. Where are you?"

"I'm out front of the house," she said, choosing not to elaborate over the phone. "Can I come over?"

"Always welcome at Casa Kayle, you know that."

"Perfect. What's your address?"

"Jackson Street Apartments, number 417. Come on up. You'll need to get buzzed in."

"Wonderful," she sighed, relieved. "I'll be over in a few. That's the one down Two Churches Road, right?"

"One and the same, girl."

"Great! See you in a minute."

She drove across town, really taking in how Newton's Grove used to look before she left for school twenty years ago. She had paid little attention when she was here last summer, what with the wedding whirlwind. So many places she remembered were gone, replaced with new businesses, or simply closed. Like the two-plex theater on the corner of Front and Snyder Streets. She saw the faded poster of some Sylvester Stallone action movie, the first in a franchise of aging action stars getting together for one last save-the-world mission. Beside that was a kid's animated movie with dinosaurs.

It struck her how she hadn't watched animated movies in years. Or any movies, for that matter. They were all boring, predictable, flashy, with superheroes and action stars trying to revive old careers. Nothing Hollywood made anymore made sense—nothing like the movies of her youth. Maggie sometimes wished she had been ten years older, growing up in the eighties when music and movies were awesome. Now, it was just blockbusters with little substance or plot. She drove through town, lost in her own memories of a place that seemed to no longer want her around, and found the road to her stepbrother's apartment complex.

Two Churches Road ran between the Methodist church on one side and the Baptist church on the other. The Baptist church had undergone renovations, and the steeple was higher than she remembered. She turned left, leaving behind the road to suburbia, with its cookie-cutter homes. It reminded her of that Malvina Reynolds song from Weeds, where everything was made of ticky-tacky, and all looked just the same. She had talked to her friend Rose several years ago when Rose was getting married and thought she'd remembered her friend telling her that they were going to move into the place. She shook her head, thinking that the once free-spirited girl had settled down to suburbia, choosing a husband and babies instead of charting a course of independence.

The Jackson Street Apartments, with their red and gray bricks, loomed on her left. Pulling into the parking lot labeled "417," her Honda chugged to a stop, emitting a puff of smoke and a few stutters.

"Gonna have to get this looked at," she muttered. "Really don't know how it made it across the country." Barely, she thought. She had almost run out of oil in Raleigh. If she hadn't seen the oil light, she would've broken down halfway to Newton's Grove. And that would have been bad. "Just a few more months, girl, hang on." She patted the dashboard, then got out, looking up at the sunny sky.

After a few minutes, she found his building and buzzed the number. It clicked, and the gate opened. She headed up to his apartment and knocked on the door. After a moment, Kayle opened it.

"Hey, sweetie, come on in!" He gave her a big hug and ushered her inside. His apartment was typical: a living area, a bar separating the kitchen and dining space, and a sliding door that opened onto a small porch with gray railings. Down the hall were two bedrooms and a bathroom. "What are you doing back in town?"

"I had a few months between jobs and figured I'd come back for the holidays," she said. Better to leave it at that, she thought.

Resting on his white leather couch, they sat opposite a white entertainment center housing a sizable flat-screen TV. "Want something to drink?" he asked, heading to the fridge. She noticed it was well-stocked when he opened it, and her stomach growled. She couldn't remember the last time she had eaten. Was it a fast-food biscuit hours ago?

"What have you got to eat?" she asked. "I'm starving."

"I was about to make a salad with grilled chicken breast. You want one?"

"Great," she said. She remembered how much she liked him when they met a few months ago. He was three years older than her, with long black hair tied in a man bun. She could see the toned muscles in his chest and legs under his tight T-shirt and black workout shorts. He would have made any woman swoon, if he were into that sort of thing.

"Din din for sis!" he said, pulling out the ingredients.

"You need help?"

"Of course not," he replied. "Let me do all the work. You talk." He handed her a craft beer, an IPA, which she popped open. It felt good to finally have someone treating her nicely, instead of snapping or insulting her. "How's my mother?"

"Not very impressive," Maggie said. "But you should know more than I do about her."

"Why would you think that?"

"Because you live in town? Don't you talk to her?"

"I don't talk to her like I used to."

"Why not?"

"Honey," he said, leveling his face with hers, "I'm gay. She doesn't approve of my 'lifestyle.' And with a name like Kayle? You know how much ribbing I got for that? Being named after a fucking vegetable?"

"And when she started that whole trad-wife, ultra-Christian thing after the wedding, I went no contact."

"Wow," she said, admiring his courage. "That takes a lot."

"I don't think so. You've met the witch."

"I just did. It only took me thirty seconds to get the picture."

He finished the salad and placed two plates on the table. Everything looked beautiful—arugula, romaine, cherry tomatoes, and other vegetables topped with perfectly sliced grilled chicken, all drizzled with honey-balsamic dressing he'd made by hand.

"This looks great," she said, spearing a piece of chicken and greens. She shoved it into her mouth like a Viking.

"Whoa," he laughed. "Someone's hungry."

"I forgot when I ate last," she said between bites. "I've been eating fast food tacos and burgers for five days while driving across the country. This is exquisite."

"Thank you," he said. She took a swig of her beer.

"So, what about you? I've talked enough."

"Not much to say. Brent and I broke up."

"When?"

"Two months ago."

"What happened?"

"He left me for some gym bro."

Maggie sighed. "Sorry to hear that."

"It happens."

"Are you okay?"

"Yeah," he replied. "I'm getting over it."

"Good."

After she ate a few more bites, he put his hand on her knee and asked, "So, what can I do for you?"

"What makes you think I wanted you to do anything for me?"

"Oh, honey, I heard it in your voice when you called me outside Mom's house. What's on your mind?" He touched her arm in a gesture of brotherly affection.

"Okay," she began. "I've got a few months before I start a new business venture. I don't know exactly what that's going to look like yet, but I know it'll be art. I got laid off from the gallery I worked at for fifteen years, so I need a place to stay until January, and I was wondering..."

"If you could stay here," he finished. He sighed, and her heart sank.

"I understand if you say no," she said quickly, setting her plate on the coffee table and standing up. "I can pay you at the end of December. I just need a place to stay, and I have no money until then. I could get a job, but it would only be for a few months, and nobody's going to hire me for that. I just don't know what to do. I was really hoping to stay with Dad and Veronica, but since I look like this, she won't even let me back into my house—my house, the one I grew up in."

"Word vomit, honey," he said gently. He stood up, walked over, and pulled her into a comforting hug. "Calm down. It's okay."

"You just don't understand," she mumbled into his shoulder. "I wouldn't have come to town if I knew this was going to happen. Now I'm stuck."

"Okay," he relented. "You can stay here. For a month or two maybe. My landlord is a stickler for guests. He watches the complex like a hawk. And don't worry about money. I've got rent and groceries covered. If you do get a job, you can pitch in with expenses, but don't stress. I'm your brother now, and I've got your back. Relax."

She tightened her hold on him. "You're the best, thank you so much. I just need a place to hang my hat for a bit before I come up with some other ideas." She was too tired from the road and hunger to think about that now, though. "Right now, I just need a shower. And a bed. Then I'll think about temp jobs and living arrangements."

That's when she heard a faint jingling sound. She looked down and saw a small black-and-white spotted cat weaving around her legs. A tiny bell hung from its pink collar, which had a tag that read, "Spot."

"Spot?" she asked, raising an eyebrow. "How original."

"Listen, hon. Don't judge. He's been my only roommate for the past few years. He'll be fine. And he likes you."

"How can you tell?"

"He doesn't come out for anyone else." Kayle scooped up the cat, kissed its head, and said, "You stay under my bed like a bashful boy, don't you?"

"Okay," she said, shrugging. "I'm stuck with my gay stepbrother and a bashful cat for a few months. Lovely." She kissed Kayle on the cheek and sat back down to finish her salad.

"Oh, it's gonna be fun," he laughed.

She smirked. "Yeah, great," she muttered, shaking her head. Two months, Maggie. Just two more months. You can do it.

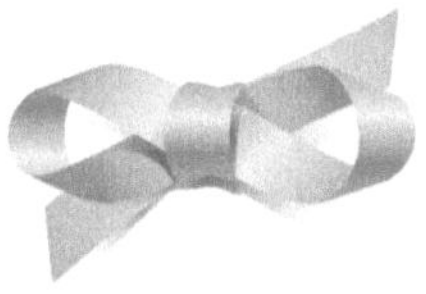

Chapter 4

Daniel

"Why do you let me win like this all the time?" Bill asked, setting the chess pieces back to their places on the chessboard in front of him. Daniel looked up from the cash register as the last customers left the store. They'd purchased several paperback Ray Bradbury novels, adding to the growing collection at home.

"What do you mean?" Daniel smiled. "You beat me fair and square."

"Bullshit."

"No joke," Daniel raised his hands. "You got me with that queen to king's rook."

"Because you let me," Bill said. "Leaving it open. Of course you'd do that. What's your angle?"

Daniel came back to him. "I'm just playing the game the way I want to play it."

"Uh huh," Bill said. He sipped his coffee, the second one today from La Perk from across the street.

"How are you doing?" Bill asked, pointing to the register.

Daniel sighed, "Not too bad, not too good. Christmas sale coming up might help out. It's October, what are you going to do?"

"Yeah," Bill agreed. "I guess I'll be heading out. You about to close up for lunch?"

"Yeah, in a minute or two."

He saw a girl with long, blond curly hair and a black outfit walking down the street toward the store. "Another customer, I guess I'll have to take it." She looked sad, and those were the easiest. Find out what they liked, take a few minutes to get to know them, and get them to smile as they hand you money for a new acquisition to put on their growing TBR.

The bell above the door dinged as she entered, looking at her phone, an absentminded look on her face. She looked around, smiled, and then walked into the store.

"Maggie?" Daniel said.

"Hey, Daniel," Maggie said, "Did ya miss me?"

"Holy shit," Daniel went around the counter to greet her. "Maggie, how are you? When did you get back into town? What's it been… since August?"

"I'm okay, I guess. Going through some stuff, but I'll be fine soon."

"What brings you back in town?" He remembered having fun with her on the night in the RV playing games with the new player, Lizzy.

"Well, you know how I was talking about the gallery opening for another great artist in LA?"

"Yeah, how did that go?"

"Turns out he wasn't that great after all. The show bombed, and my boss lost her shirt. So, we had to close up and I decided to come back to town and see what's going on now that I have a few months to kill."

"That's fantastic. Do you want to play in the game? Paulie and the guys miss you. And the video of Derrick's daughter went crazy viral, I'm sure you've seen it."

"I have," she said. "How funny is that?"

"I'm still the DM, if you want to join."

"I'd love that." She smiled. "Do you want to have dinner or something? Catch up?"

"Oh, I couldn't," he said.

"Why not?"

"I'm just… I'm just used to eating alone at this point. I wouldn't know how to carry on a conversation. You'd be bored senseless."

"Daniel, I'm a friend. Why can't you go to dinner with a friend?"

"I suppose. Sure you won't be bored?"

"I promise."

He changed the subject. "So, what brings you back into town?"

"Business stuff," she said. "And I'll leave it at that. It's a long story. Maybe I'll tell you over dinner."

"That's a deal. Did you need a book? I was about to close for lunch, but what were you looking for?"

"I had to put all my books in storage when I moved out of my apartment in LA, so I was going to start with my favorite first."

"And what's that?"

"Wuthering Heights?"

"Of course," he said. "Got all the classics back here. He started back to the shelves marked "Classics" written in sharpie marker on white construction paper. She looked up and noticed the sign.

"High class joint you're running here," she joked, pointing to the paper taped to a brown shelving unit.

"It's a used book store," he shrugged. "Cassie used to replace those all the time when they looked worn down. It's been a while."

"So maybe you need someone around the place to help you spruce it up again. Give the place a revamp, maybe get some more customers in."

"Maggie," he said gravely. "It's Newton's Crossing. There's only so many people who're going to come to a used book store and gem shop."

"You'd be surprised. I'm seeing a lot of girls on TikTok that would love a store like this."

"That's the last thing I need, social media."

"Oh, stop being such a boomer," she laughed. "Hire me, I'd be perfect for the job."

"What job?"

"Social media manager and brand rep," she answered, taking the sign down and balling it in her fist. "And a general sprucer upper."

"I don't have a lot of money I could pay you," he said. "I don't know."

"Try it out for a week. You don't like me? Send me packing."

"You're very forward, you know that?"

"So I've been told." She looked along the shelves, wiped away some dust, and found a copy of Wuthering Heights. There it is." She pulled it out, blew off some dust, and showed him her finger, smudged with gray dirt from the shelf. "So, what do you say?"

Daniel sighed and asked, "When can you start?"

"That's the spirit, Danny boy." She smiled. "How about in a couple of days. I have to find a place to live first."

"Why can't you go home?" he asked. He took the book from her and went to the register.

"An even longer story," she followed him to the front of the store, and saw the shrine he'd laid out with Cassandra's smiling picture, the gems, and other odd bits of memorabilia resting on the stool covered by white and yellow striped fabric.

"Maybe you can tell me over dinner," he said with a smile. He put the book in a white Cassandra's paper bag and handed it to her. "It's on me."

"Thanks, but let me pay for it."

"I couldn't charge an employee," he said. "Oh, that reminds me." He went to the printer next to the counter and pulled out a piece of paper. "Give me your name and phone number and an address and I'll get it to my accountant."

"Sure," she went into her silver purse for a pen and started writing. He pulled out his reading glasses and looked as she wrote her name.

"Magpie?" he asked. She looked up at him with a smile.

"Maggie," she chuckled at the mistake. "Need new glasses there, Danny boy?"

He took them off and looked. They were 2x. "I guess I need some better ones."

She slid the paper back to him. He looked and saw no address. "Let me know if you find something or not," he said. "I might be able to help you out. It's a last-ditch kind of thing, but don't let me hear you're homeless."

"I'm sure I'll figure it out," she said. "I have a few months at Kayle's apartment. But I'll let you know."

"So, dinner tonight, there's always Angelo's."

"I like Italian," she said. "Lord, I love their chicken parm."

"It's the best," he said. "It's settled. I close up at six. See you there at seven?"

"I will," she said. "This'll be fun." He noticed a sweet flirtation in her eyes, the way she looked at him. His heart thumped. She went to hug him again, and he let her. It was a brief, friendly hug, but she squeezed him tight at the end.

"Yes," he said. "I'm sure it will." he released her, and she went to the door.

She stepped out, saying, "See you at seven, Danny boy."

"It's a date, Magpie," he said. The door closed, and she walked away. Then she turned, looked through the glass at him, and waved.

He looked around at the store, empty of customers, and said to Bill, "Well that was a helluva thing."

Bill gave him a knowing look. "Uh huh."

Chapter 5

Maggie

"What the fuck?" she yelled, trying the key in her Honda for the third time. Click. Nothing. It was dead. She leaned back in the driver's seat. "Why is my life falling apart just two months before everything is supposed to get better!?" She screamed at the ceiling. Pounding the steering wheel with angry fists, she then settled back into the seat. "Okay, let's try this again."

She turned the key.

Click.

Nothing.

"FUCK!" she screamed. "SHIT! SHIT! SHIT!"

She calmed herself, breathing in and out like her yoga teacher in LA had taught her. In through the nose, out through the mouth. Glancing at her phone, it was six-thirty. Daniel was probably already on his way to the restaurant. She found his name in the contacts and hit send.

He answered on the third ring. "Hey, how's it going? We're still on for tonight, right?"

"Yes," she said. She could hear the shower in the background. Either he was just getting out, or just getting in—either way, she couldn't help but imagine this handsome older guy naked in his bathroom. She cleared her throat. "Only..."

"Only... what?" he asked.

"My fucking car won't start. I think I need a jump." In more ways than one, she thought to herself.

"Okay," he said. She heard the shower turn off. "Where are you? Maybe I can help."

"Oh, you don't need to do that."

"Magpie, you're a friend. Where are you?"

"At my brother's apartment complex," she explained with a sigh. "Jackson Street Apartments. Down Two Churches Road."

"I know it, yes."

"Sorry about this."

"It's no problem. I'm a sucker for a damsel in distress. I'll be over in a few minutes."

"Well, I'm definitely in distress."

"I'll be right there. Hang tight."

"Thanks, Danny boy."

"No problem, Magpie."

What a way to start a date with the guy she'd been crushing on for half her life. Here she was, all dolled up, and now she was about to get dirty. She got out of the car, opened the hood, and leaned against the Honda, trying to look cute in her green flouncy skirt, crochet top, and breezy black wrap. Maybe I can salvage this night after all, she thought.

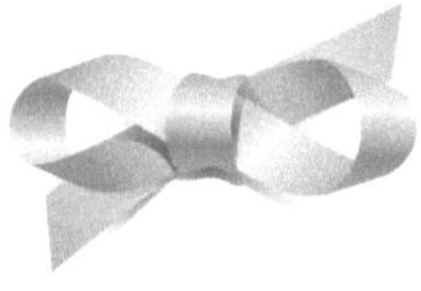

Chapter 6

Daniel

He dressed in jeans and a t-shirt, knowing he'd be doing car repairs tonight instead of fine dining. It was okay, though. He'd eaten a few hours earlier—something from the fridge that didn't look stale and was just barely edible. He needed to get rid of all the fast food and Angelo's containers piling up, but he knew he wouldn't. It would take a woman's touch to clean it up, and there hadn't been a woman in his life for five years. Not since Cass.

He got into his car and drove to Jackson Street.

The street was at a crossroads. To the left was the road leading to White Pines Homes and Sycamore Park, and to the right was Jackson Street East. On one side of the street stood a stately Methodist church with a red brick exterior and a high steeple. Across from it was an even statelier Baptist church, with clean whitewashed siding and an even taller steeple. It looked like the Baptists had won the steeple war.

Over the years, both churches had undergone renovations, but a hurricane several years ago destroyed the steeple of the Baptist church. After raising the funds for a new one, they made it two feet taller than the Methodist steeple. This was a point of pride for Reverend Doctor Ken Lightman, who had once preached that the sun rising on the tallest point of the city meant God looked favorably upon his church. That was before a scandal involving an underage parishioner, her mother, and the cousin of the same had taken him down. Some said it was all three at once, but those rumors were highly suspect.

Chuckling to himself about small-town gossip, Daniel drove down the road until he saw the Jackson Street Apartments. This was a passion project of Jake Marleigh, a local developer, and real estate investor—and the owner of the bookstore. It was a nice, two-story red brick complex of several buildings, each with luxury three-bedroom apartments. The landscaping was immaculate, with oaks and pine trees shielding it mostly from the road.

He pulled around to Maggie's apartment and saw her leaning against her car, the hood already up, waiting for him. The setting sun blazed through her hair, and when she turned to look at him, it illuminated her curls, highlighting the blue-dyed strands. His heart thumped. *Dammit, what am I doing?* he thought. He breathed deeply a couple of times. *Stay focused, Dan. She's your daughter's friend. A younger woman. Too many things could go wrong here.*

He shook his head, composed himself, and got out of the car.

Maggie walked over and they shared a quick hug. "Hey," he said. "So, show me the damage."

She led him to the front of the car, and he saw the problem right away. He sighed. "Mag, when was the last time you looked at your battery terminals?"

"Never?" she gave him a blank look. "I don't know."

"Look," he said. She came around to the front of the Honda. He pointed at the battery, corroded with blue and white gunk around the terminals. "How did you even start this thing?"

"It just started," she said, frowning. "It took a few tries, but it always started."

"And it never occurred to you to check under the hood?"

"The last guy who did anything to it said it didn't look too bad."

"When was that?"

"Two, maybe three years ago?" she shrugged.

Daniel let out an exasperated sigh. "And where's your oil cap?"

She glanced at the engine. "Oh... where did that go?"

"Yeah, where did it go?" he asked, his patience wearing thin.

"Somewhere near Raleigh, I guess?" She put a hand on his arm and stooped to look closer at the motor. "That's the last time I put oil in it."

"And you didn't think to put the cap back on?"

"I was in a hurry, and it was dark on the side of the road."

"You don't put oil in your car on the side of the road in the dark," he said, his frustration clear. "You do it when you buy it at the station or have someone change it every three thousand miles. Didn't your dad teach you any of this?"

"He's a lawyer, Dan," she explained dryly. "We just took our cars in when they needed stuff like that."

Daniel sighed again and pulled the hood down with a bang. She jumped.

"What the hell?" she exclaimed.

"Get in the car," he said, pointing to his Acura. "We're going to AutoZone."

"What about dinner?" she asked. "I'm starving."

"This will only take a few minutes. I'm buying you a new battery and some terminals, and I'll put them on tomorrow."

"Aww, that's sweet. I'll pay you back with my first paycheck." She got into his neat blue Acura and settled into the passenger seat. "This is nice."

"I keep it that way," he said. "And I stay on top of the maintenance too, unlike some people I know."

"What can I say," she smiled sweetly at him, "I'm a girl."

"That's no excuse." He started the car, and they pulled out of the apartment complex, heading downtown to AutoZone. He hoped Daveon was working tonight—he always got a good deal. Daveon had been a customer at the bookstore for a long time, ever since his mom brought him in when he was eleven. The kid had fallen in love with The Hobbit and had read every novel about Middle-earth.

Daveon had even told Daniel about the fantasy books he was writing. Daniel had promised him that if they ever got published, he'd do a signing at the bookstore. Now Daveon was twenty-two, married, with a seven-month-old baby and another kid on the way. Daniel doubted he'd ever finish that book now.

A few minutes later, they arrived at the black-and-orange AutoZone on Market Street.

"What's up, Dan?" said the young man behind the counter as they walked in. "How's it hangin'?"

"Daveon," Daniel shook his hand. "Good to see you. How's the book coming?"

"Three chapters to go, big guy," Daveon said with a huge smile. "Janelle's letting me write at night after the baby goes to sleep. It's been going great."

"Good to hear." Daniel always loved hearing success stories from his customers. Daveon had it tough growing up, with a single mom and a deadbeat dad who drifted in and out of his life. But the kid had persevered, with a little help from Daniel and his bookstore. "I can't wait to read it."

"Man, you'd dig it the most."

"I'm sure I will."

"So, what can I get you tonight?"

"I need some battery cables and a battery for a—" he looked over at Maggie. "What year is it?"

"Two thousand four," she said. "Honda Accord."

Daveon typed on the keyboard, clicked the mouse, and nodded. "Yeah, we've got what you need. Anything else?"

"An oil cap for the same car," Daniel said, glancing at Maggie.

She stuck her tongue out like a mischievous child.

He smiled. "Don't be a brat."

"What if I want to?" She winked at him.

"And stop flirting."

"What if I don't want to?"

Daveon chuckled. "I'll grab that stuff for you. Looks like you two need some time alone anyway."

"Don't leave me alone with her," Daniel joked. "Please."

"Sorry, old man," Daveon shrugged. "Gotta head to the back room."

"Go ahead," Maggie said, grinning. "I won't attack him here. The lights are too bright."

"There you go, Dan," Daveon laughed as he walked toward the shelves. "You're safe."

"So you say." Daniel glanced at Maggie again, and she stuck out her tongue once more.

Half an hour later, they pulled up to Angelo's. It was 8:15, but the "Open" sign was off.

"That's odd," Daniel said. "They usually don't close until nine."

"Damn," Maggie muttered. "And I'm starving."

"Okay, I've got a solution. Let's just go back to my place. I've got some pasta and sauce; we can whip something up. It'll only take a few minutes."

"Dinner at your place?" Her eyes lit up with a bright smile. "Sign me up."

"I'll take that as a yes." They drove to his house on Bayshore Lane. Halfway there, she placed a hand on his thigh.

"Thank you," she said softly. "For everything. You're a lifesaver, Danny boy."

"It's no problem," he replied. "I'd do it for anyone."

"I know." She gave his thigh a gentle squeeze. "That's what makes you so attractive."

"Maggie," he said, glancing down at her hand on his leg. He met her gaze. A part of him wanted her hand to stay there, but he listened to the better part of his conscience. Gently, he lifted her hand off his thigh and returned it to her lap. "You're welcome."

They arrived at his house, a two-story neo-colonial ranch home, typical of the neighborhood. He went to the passenger door and opened it for her.

"Always a gentleman," she said, smiling.

"Yes," he replied. "For anyone, though, not just you."

"Aww, and here I thought I was special."

"You are," he said. He thought of something else to say but stopped himself. He didn't want to encourage her flirting. That wouldn't do at all. He'd already indulged it more than he should have. His mind continuously wandered back to the memory of the eighteen-year-old girl in his kitchen, flirting years ago, and the intense taboo it held at the time. Now was no different.

He unlocked the door, and they went in.

"Still the same living room furniture," she remarked, noticing the brown leather sofa and easy chair she remembered from so long ago. "Don't you ever redecorate?"

"There's no need," he answered, heading toward the kitchen. "Everything is where I like it."

He went to a cabinet, opened it up, and pulled out a box of pasta and a jar of Alfredo sauce. "There's probably some hamburger in the fridge."

She opened the fridge and peeked in. "Daniel," she said, disappointed. "There are only takeout containers and some yogurt." She picked up the yogurt container and grimaced. "From a year ago."

"Huh," he came over and glanced at it. "Must've been from when I was on a health kick. Throw it away."

"And the takeout food?"

"I'll get to that later." He rummaged through the lower cabinets and found a saucepan. He turned on a burner on the oven, its surface caked with grease and cooking crumbs. "Sorry about the state of the place. I wasn't expecting company."

"That's fine," she said, heading to the pantry. "Got any chips or crackers? I'm really hungry."

"Don't ruin your appetite. But if you must, there's some Pringles in there, I think."

She found a red Pringles can, opened it, and saw a few broken chips at the bottom. She fished one out, put it in her mouth, and grimaced. "Ew." She checked the expiration date. "Three years old, Danny boy."

"That old, huh? Throw them away, then."

She tossed the can into the trash. "How old is that spaghetti?"

"A couple of weeks, I guess?" He went to check, but she picked up the box first, looked inside, and gasped.

"Weevils." She immediately threw it away. Daniel felt a flush of embarrassment. He had wanted to impress her, but everything about the night was falling apart.

"Listen," he said, defeated. "Maybe we should try again another night."

"No, it's fine. I'm sure you have another box of noodles somewhere. But first," she looked at the Alfredo jar. "Really?"

"What?"

"It's two years old, Daniel."

"No, it can't be." He took the jar from her and checked the date. Sure enough, it expired two years ago. "Shit." He handed it back to her, resting his hands on the counter, his head hanging in frustration.

She put the jar down and went over to him, wrapping her arms around his waist from behind.

"Hey," she whispered. "It's okay. We'll figure something else out."

"It's not that," he said, tensing at her touch.

"Then what is it?"

"I can change a lightbulb. I can fix plumbing. I can replace a car battery. I can do a million things right—run a store, build a treehouse, for crying out loud," his voice escalated, growing frantic and angry. "But I can't even buy groceries!"

He grabbed the jar of Alfredo sauce and hurled it at the wall, where it shattered, spraying moldy sauce everywhere. Maggie jumped, startled. She backed away, her mouth open in shock.

He rushed to her, grabbing her shoulders. "Jesus, I'm so sorry. I didn't mean—" He broke down, collapsing into her arms. She embraced him, cradling his head against her chest.

"It's okay," she whispered, soothing him with gentle shushing sounds. "Let it go." She wiped away one of his tears as he looked at her, his face softening.

"It's stupid, I know," he said, calming down. "It just hits me sometimes. When I least expect it. Let me clean this up."

He went to the pantry to grab a broom and dustpan.

She placed a hand on his back. "Anytime you want to talk, I'm here."

"Thank you." He started sweeping up the glass and sauce.

She pulled out her phone. "Looks like it's Domino's, then." Minutes later, she was ordering. Daniel didn't put up a fight, giving vague answers as she asked what he wanted. In the end, she ordered a large pepperoni and mushroom pizza with cheesy bread and a two-liter Coke.

By the time she finished, he had cleaned up the mess on the floor and wall. He still felt shaken but her patience and understanding touched him.

"Thanks for being here tonight," he said. "I really appreciate it."

"You bought me stuff to fix my car, Danny boy. I should be thanking you."

"So, what do you want to do while we wait for the pizza?"

"Let's watch a movie. What's your favorite?"

"Blazing Saddles," he said. "Yours?"

"Mean Girls," she replied. "I've never seen Blazing Saddles."

"Oh, you're in for a treat. It's the most offensive movie ever, and there's no way it could be made today."

"I'm up for that. Then, after it's over, how about we watch mine?"

"Let's save that for another night."

"We've got a deal," she smiled. "Another night sounds nice."

Twenty minutes later, with pizza, breadsticks, and soda, they sat down to watch Gene Wilder, a black sheriff, and the townspeople of Rock Ridge defeat the evil machinations of Harvey Korman and his gang of misfit goons.

"That was the most offensive movie ever," she said, grinning. "I loved every minute of it."

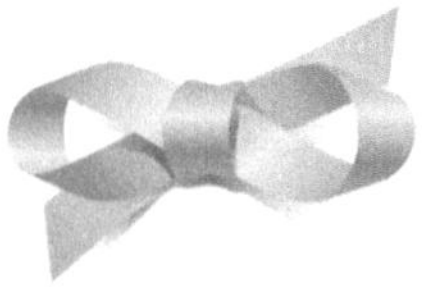

Chapter 7

Maggie

Maggie tugged at her tie-dyed T-shirt, feeling the fabric stretch against her skin as she glanced up at the bookstore. Her black jeans, frayed at the hems, brushed against her Converse as she shifted her weight nervously. She pulled her ponytail a little tighter, took a deep breath, and smiled as she stepped inside. She had a feeling she'd be cleaning today and dressed down. If she were selling books, alongside Daniel, she would have worn something prettier. She hoped it would be okay to wear this outfit on her first day.

The familiar smell of old paper and dust filled the air, welcoming her. She always loved that smell, ever since she was a kid visiting her first library with her grandmother when she was seven. Now she would be smelling it every day. If there was a candle that had that smell, she thought, she would buy every one she could get her hands on. Bookstore smell always reminded her of Nana and how the old woman would give her fifty cents to buy kids' books or comic books when they went together.

Behind the counter, Bill and Daniel were hunched over a chessboard, locked in their daily game. The sight of them bickering like an old married couple made her grin.

"Ready for duty, boss," Maggie called playfully as she approached them.

Daniel looked up, a smile already forming on his lips. Bill's eyes sparkled as he leaned back in his chair, clearly pleased with himself after taking Daniel's rook. He had two pawns and a knight ready to trap Daniel's king. The game was as good as over.

"Once again, you are about to wipe the floor with me," Daniel said, sitting back in defeat. "I should probably take care of the new girl, anyway."

Bill smirked. "Don't worry. Take care of the new kid. I won't cheat."

"You do every other day. What makes today different?" Daniel raised an eyebrow.

Bill grinned, looking up from the board. "I only cheat because you let me. But I'll try not to today, don't want Mags here to get the wrong impression of me."

Maggie laughed. "Too late, Bill. I already have the wrong impression of you."

Bill chuckled, shaking his head. "I like this one. Keep her around. She's fun."

Maggie stuck out her tongue at him. Bill did the same back, and she couldn't help but laugh at how at ease she already felt. It was going to be fun working with these two stodgy old men for the next few months, arguing like the two old guys on the Muppets show.

Bill picked up his empty coffee cup with the La Perk logo and shook it. "I'm off to get a refill. Anyone want anything?"

"Everything bagel for me," Maggie said. "Please."

"Blueberry muffin," Daniel added. "Janet's makes the best muffins every morning."

With a final glance at the board, Bill stood and headed for the door. "I'll be back." He tried to give an Arnold Schwarzenegger impression. Maggie laughed and Daniel just shook his head.

"Not that good, I know," Bill said, opening the door. "I'll try harder next time."

"It was great," Maggie said. "Can't wait to hear more."

"Don't get him started. He'll be insufferable."

He shot Daniel the middle finger as the door shut behind him, and Daniel smiled. They watched him jog as fast as he could across the street, avoiding mid-morning traffic.

As soon as he left, the store fell into a comfortable silence. Maggie glanced at Daniel, feeling a brief tension pass between them. She could see he was thinking, maybe about what to do with her on her first day. Or maybe something else entirely. His gaze lingered on her for a moment longer than she expected.

"Alright, boss," she said, breaking the silence with a grin. "What's first?"

"Follow me," Daniel pushed himself up from his chair.

They walked through the aisles, past shelves overflowing with books—many of them dusty and cluttered. Maggie noticed duct tape holding some of the shelves together, the carpet looking like it hadn't been vacuumed in weeks, maybe longer.

"How do people find anything in here?" she asked, raising an eyebrow.

Daniel chuckled. "I'm usually helping them."

They reached the back of the store, where a massive old freight elevator stood, its chains rusted, and a sign that said "Out of Order" taped across the platform. Daniel pointed at it. "Used to be for moving appliances upstairs when this place was a retail store. Now it's just... decoration, I guess."

Maggie smiled, loving the odd charm of it all.

Daniel led her to a mop and bucket in the corner near two back doors. "There's a hose out back you can use to fill the bucket. We've got plenty of cleaners here—Clorox, glass cleaner, Murphy's Oil Soap. You can use these paper towels from Bennett's Hardware."

She picked up a bottle of Murphy's Oil Soap, gave it a shake, and smirked. "I'll do more than just dust."

"Just don't get the books wet," Daniel warned, a hint of amusement in his voice.

"Don't worry, Danny boy," she replied with a wink. "I know what I'm doing."

Their conversation was easy, the banter flowing naturally. Daniel was being courteous, but there was a softness to his tone she hadn't noticed before. As if something was shifting between them.

"Maggie," Daniel said, pausing for a moment, his voice thoughtful. "I'm really glad you're here. This place has needed a woman's touch for a long time."

Maggie felt a warmth spread through her chest at his words. She stepped forward and gave him the briefest of hugs, feeling him stiffen slightly before relaxing. "Glad to be here," she said softly. "I think we'll have some fun together."

"I hope we do," he replied, a small smile playing on his lips.

Before the moment could linger too long, the door swung open and Bill returned with a brown paper bag and two coffee cups. "Got the goods," he announced. He handed the bagel to Maggie and the muffin to Daniel.

Daniel took the muffin with a grateful nod. "So, how is 'she'?" he teased.

"Who's 'she'?" Maggie asked, raising an eyebrow.

Daniel smiled, explaining, "Bill has a crush on one of the new women who works at La Perk. Charlotte, right?"

Bill sighed, rolling his eyes. "I don't have a crush."

"He sends her flowers every week," Daniel added.

"Not flowers," Bill corrected. "Just half a dozen roses. She doesn't know they're from me, but I see her smile when they're delivered, so that's nice."

Maggie couldn't help but smile at the image. "Why don't you just tell her?"

Bill glanced at her, then at Daniel. "Look at me. I'm overweight and half bald. The only things I've got going for me are wit, money, and charm."

Daniel snorted. "You have charm?"

Bill shot him a playful glare. "Isn't that why you keep me around?"

"No, I keep you around to beat me at chess."

"I only beat you because you let me."

"Yeah, but it's fun."

Bill turned to Maggie, flashing her a wink. "This guy used to be a chess champion in high school. He knows all the openings and defenses but lets me win. I don't get it."

"You're pretty good yourself," Daniel added.

"That's bull," Bill said with a laugh. "I can't even beat the computer on easy. But I'll take it." He moved his knight, triumphantly announcing, "Checkmate. Set 'em up again."

Daniel sighed dramatically. "Oh darn, he beat me again."

Maggie watched the two banter, her mouth full of bagel. Daniel caught her eye, gave her a quick wink, and she winked back, grinning.

"Alright," Maggie said, brushing crumbs from her hands. "These shelves aren't going to clean themselves."

Bill grinned. "If they did, that'd be a miracle."

Daniel chuckled. "If you did your job, I wouldn't have had to hire her."

"I don't work here, remember?" Bill shot back.

Daniel sighed, shaking his head. "One of these days, I'm going to fire you."

Bill crossed his arms, mock-serious. "I've got tenure. You wouldn't."

Daniel smiled softly. "No, I wouldn't."

As the conversation faded, Maggie got to work. She started with the shelves, dusting off layers that had clearly settled for years, maybe longer. She put books back in alphabetical order, organizing as she went. Every now and then, she glanced at Daniel, who had resumed his game with Bill.

He looked... different than she remembered. Older, sure, but in a way that made him more handsome. The sadness around his eyes, though, still lingered. That bothered her. She wondered if it was something she could help with, something she could heal over time.

Later, just before closing, Daniel walked up to her, surveying her progress. He smiled, genuinely impressed. "You've done an amazing job. Thank you for this."

Maggie wiped her hands on her jeans, feeling accomplished. "You're welcome."

"How about we go out and celebrate? You, me, and Bill?" Daniel suggested.

Bill shook his head. "Can't. I've got a date."

"With who? Vanna White?" Daniel teased.

"You got it," Bill replied with a smirk. "You two have fun."

Daniel turned back to Maggie. "I need to go home and change. You probably do too, right?"

Maggie glanced down at her shirt, now smeared with dust, and her hands, wrinkled from cleaning. "Yeah, I look like I've been through a war zone. Meet me at Angelo's at seven?"

"Sounds perfect. We'll get that chicken parm we missed last night."

"Good," Maggie said with a grin. "But I could go for another pizza."

"Then pizza it is." Daniel smiled. "See you at seven."

"See you then, Danny boy," Maggie teased.

"Later, Magpie," he called back, a warmth in his voice that made her smile.

Maggie walked out of the store, her heart light. She could hear Daniel locking up behind her, and as she reached her car, she saw him walking toward his own. Their eyes met across the street, and she waved. He waved back, shaking his head with a small smile.

God, you're cute, Mr. Man, she thought to herself as her orange Honda Accord roared to life with a struggling whirr. Too cute.

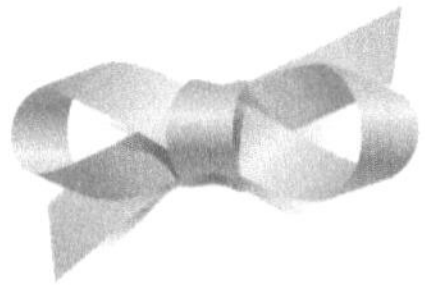

Chapter 8

Maggie

She had just stepped out of the shower when she heard a knock at the door. She quickly wrapped herself in a robe and secured her wet hair in a towel before answering. *Shit, who's this at nine-thirty in the morning,* she thought.

Standing in the doorway was a man with a smug grin plastered on his face. He gave her a once-over and smirked. "Not the greeting I was expecting, but I'll take it," he said, leering suggestively.

Maggie crossed her arms and stared at him coldly. "Can I help you?"

The man faltered, caught off guard by her piercing gaze. "Uh, yes—sorry about that, I was just joking, of course."

"Of course," she said dryly. "But my question stands."

He cleared his throat, trying to recover. "I'm looking for Kayle... uh, Kayle Dover?"

"He's here," she replied. "And you are?"

"The landlord," he said, puffing out his chest. "I've come about the rent."

"I believe Kayle already paid for this month."

"Oh, he has. This is about going forward." The man raised an eyebrow. "And you are?"

"Margaret. His stepsister."

The landlord's face lit up with interest. "Well, that's interesting news."

Maggie's eyes narrowed. "How is it interesting?"

Just then, Kayle emerged from his bedroom, rubbing his eyes like he'd just woken up. "Hey, Mags, what's going on?"

"This guy's here about the rent," Maggie said, jerking her thumb toward the landlord. "Sorry, I know you worked late, I was trying to stay quiet."

"It's okay," Kayle kissed her on the forehead. He turned to the man and frowned. "I already paid for this month."

The landlord nodded. "It's not that you haven't paid. It's about the upcoming increase, for you and everyone here at Jackson Street."

Kayle blinked in confusion. "But I have a lease—it's good until next July."

"Yes, well, that will need to change starting in January."

"Wait, who are you?" Kayle asked, now fully awake.

"Oh, sorry, where are my manners," the man said, flashing a greasy smile. "I'm Ellis Marleigh, Jake's son."

Kayle crossed his arms. "Where's Jake? I usually deal with him."

Ellis's expression turned somber, though Maggie could tell it was all for show. "Unfortunately, Jake's in poor health. He had a stroke not long ago and can't handle any of his responsibilities. I've taken over the business."

"I'm sorry to hear that," Kayle said sincerely. "Is there anything I can do?"

"Well," Ellis said, his eyes flicking to Maggie. "The best thing you can do is explain this situation."

Kayle glanced at Maggie. "My stepsister's visiting for the holidays."

"Holidays?" Ellis raised an eyebrow. "It's the beginning of November. How many holidays is she staying for?"

"Until New Year's," Maggie said evenly.

Ellis's smile grew. "Well, then, it looks like you have a roommate. A female roommate, I might add."

"And what exactly does that mean?" Maggie asked, her tone sharp.

Ellis straightened, his voice dripping with condescension. "According to the lease, this is a single-occupancy dwelling."

"But there are two bedrooms," Kayle pointed out.

"Yes, but you signed a single-occupancy lease. That means having another person live here constitutes cohabitation."

Kayle blinked. "Cohabitation? Isn't that for, like, boyfriend-girlfriend situations?"

Ellis's smirk deepened. "Isn't that what this is?"

Maggie and Kayle exchanged glances and burst into laughter. "Are you serious?" Maggie said between chuckles.

Kayle wiped his eyes. "No, no, no, it's not like that at all."

Ellis's face remained impassive. "Well, in this day and age, it's not unusual for step-siblings to, you know... get along. It's not unheard of—if you catch my meaning."

Maggie shot him a disgusted look. "Oh, I catch your meaning. But as if I were to do that with him?" She pointed at Kayle.

Kayle shook his head, grimacing. "Dude, I don't even like her—or her gender, for that matter. Honestly, I'd be more into you, if you weren't such a stick-up-the-ass."

Ellis flushed, taken aback by the jab. He quickly regained his composure. "Be that as it may," he said, his tone now cold and businesslike, "it still counts as cohabitation. Which means I'll need to raise the rent and have you sign a new lease."

"I'm allowed to have guests, you know," Kayle retorted.

"Yes, guests—who stay for a week or two. But if she's staying for two months, we'll need to adjust the rent accordingly."

"You can't do that!" Kayle protested.

Ellis flashed a slick salesman's smile. "Oh, I can—and I will. Starting in December, your rent will double."

Kayle's jaw dropped. "That's $2,400! That's highway robbery!"

"It is what it is," Ellis said with a shrug. "And if I don't have it by December 1st, you're out."

Kayle crossed his arms. "You can't do that. There are laws protecting renters."

Ellis chuckled darkly. "You think I care about that? I could call the sheriff and have you out today if I wanted. Be glad I'm feeling generous."

Kayle fumed. "But you can't—"

"I just told you I will," Ellis interrupted smoothly. "$2,400 by December 1st." He paused, as if in thought, then smiled a greasy salesman's smile. "Or, I can be more lenient: if your stepsister's out of the apartment by then, the rent will stay the same. Otherwise, I'm sure you two can scrape together the money. If not, there are plenty of applicants who would gladly pay that amount without hesitation."

Kayle, clearly defeated, muttered, "We'll talk about it."

"Good," Ellis said, his voice sickeningly sweet. "I'm glad we see eye to eye." He extended his hand to Maggie. "Nice meeting you."

Maggie looked down at his hand, then back up at his smug face. "Maggie," she said coolly. "Maggie Thorne." And with that, she slammed the door in his face.

They heard a chuckle from behind the door and Maggie turned to her brother. "Shit! What are we going to do?"

Kayle sighed, went to the couch and sat down heavily. "I don't know. How much are you making at that bookstore job?"

"Not enough for twelve hundred dollars."

"Shit," Kayle said. "There has to be a law or something. I have to find my lease. Goddammit!" He stood up and went to his bedroom.

"I can move out," she said as he walked down the hall. "I didn't mean for any of this to happen."

Kayle turned on her and said, "No. There has to be something we can do. It's not like you're moving in. Let me read the lease."

"You didn't read it when you signed it?"

"No, I just signed, I took their word for it. Besides, it was all boilerplate. Party of the first part and all that shit."

"You're supposed to read it before you sign it."

"Do you read the terms and conditions before you hit accept and move on?" Kayle asked smugly. Maggie cocked her head to the side and rolled her eyes.

"No," she said. "I get your point."

"Now where is it?" He went into his bedroom, with tan walls and a mattress and box springs on the floor next to a table made from a couple of milk crates. There were clothes on the floor, most of them from his job, Harvey's Bar and Bistro, where he closed most nights as a bartender.

"Don't you ever clean up in here?" she asked, turning her nose at the stale beer and man smell of his room.

"I do it on weekdays when I don't work."

"I just thought you guys were neater, that's all," she joked.

"Darling, gays can be slobs sometimes too, you know."

"I'm joking, don't look so hurt."

"I know sweetie, I'm joking back," he went to the closet, and a pile of clothing spilled out on the floor in front of him. "This is going to be impossible." He sat on the bed, his face in his hands.

"It's okay, just go to the office on Monday and get a copy, they have to let you see it. Or I will."

"No, they'll only give it to me. I'll do it."

"Okay, in the meantime, I'll look for another place to stay. It can't be so hard to find a friend to bunk with." She thought of Daniel and thought she might appeal to his nature. He does have a big house after all, and she'd seen how he looked at her sometimes. And she liked how he looked at her all the time. "I'll ask my boss. Maybe he'll give me an idea."

"Whatever you say," Kayle agreed. "But if nothing happens, I can come up with the money. I just have to sell some investments, but it shouldn't be too hard. I was hoping to avoid that, but for family, I will."

"Don't do that yet. Let me talk to Dan, see what he can come up with."

"Good luck with that,"

"I think I'll be very lucky," she grinned.

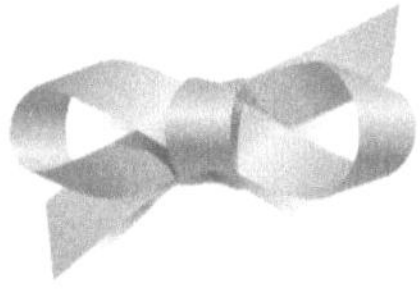

Chapter 9

Daniel

It was the day after Ellis had shown up at Kayle's apartment, and Maggie had been quiet all morning. She'd been agonizing about how to bring up her living situation with Daniel, unsure how to tell him what was weighing on her. Throughout the morning, she'd only given one-word answers to his questions and kept out of his way.

Around lunchtime, Daniel finally suggested, "How about we go grab some sandwiches? You've been working hard, and I'd like to treat you."

Maggie shook her head, "No, it's okay. I'll just eat in the car."

"It's too chilly out for that. C'mon, let me take you to lunch. You've been doing a great job, and I need to reward my favorite employee."

She couldn't help but chuckle. "I'm your only employee, Danny boy."

"And that's why you're my favorite."

He smiled, clearly trying to lighten the mood, and she appreciated the effort. "There it is," he said, "I was hoping to see a smile from you today."

"I'm sorry. I've just... been a little on edge."

His smile faded slightly. "What do you mean? What's wrong?"

Maggie hesitated before answering, her voice low. "I got some bad news yesterday, and I'm still trying to process it."

Daniel looked concerned. "Okay, then let's do this—come to the deli with me, and tell me over lunch. Sometimes a good listener is all you need."

She shook her head. "I need more than a good listener."

"What do you mean?"

"Oh, Daniel... why are you so good to me?" She sighed, her emotions starting to bubble over.

"It's just the way I am," he said with a reassuring smile. "But seriously, what's on your mind?"

Maggie looked down, wringing her hands. "It's just... I hate to ask this. You've already done so much by giving me a job. I don't want to cross any lines or overstep, and I know you were just being nice when you offered, so I don't know..." She rambled, her voice shaky.

"Hey, hey," he interrupted gently, "What's going on, Magpie?"

She took a deep breath. "I need a place to stay... and I remember you saying you might be able to put me up for a bit. It's only for a few months, just until I get back on my feet. But—oh, forget it!" She turned away, frustrated.

"It's fine," Daniel said calmly, stepping closer. "Actually, I think I've got an idea. But you'll have to help me with it."

She looked at him, confused. "What do you mean?"

He smiled, "Come with me," and took her hand.

Maggie let herself be led to the back of the store, up a set of creaky wooden stairs to a loft area. The space was cluttered with boxes of books, old furniture, and dusty shelves. He walked over to one of the covered windows and tore down the paper, letting in a sliver of light.

The loft had potential. A bathroom sat in the corner with its door slightly ajar. He opened it for her to peek in—a bit dingy, but functional. "It's not much," he admitted, "but it'll do in a pinch."

There was a small kitchenette with an ancient refrigerator humming in the corner. The cabinets were old, one door hanging crooked, and the fixtures looked like they'd been installed in the fifties.

"If you help me fix this place up," he said with a grin, "it's yours."

Maggie's eyes widened in surprise. "Really?"

"Sure, no problem. We'll call it part of your pay."

"Get out of here," she said with a laugh.

"Seriously. It's only for a few months, right?"

"Yeah, but..." She hesitated. "I was kind of hoping to move into your house."

He shook his head. "Nah, this is better. Believe me."

"Yeah, I've seen your house. It's a mess."

He laughed. "Well, so is this. But it can be your mess—if you help me clean it up."

She looked at him, tears welling in her eyes. "Deal, boss," she said, extending her hand.

He shook it, and for a moment, they held each other's gaze, their hands lingering in the handshake. "Welcome home," he said with a warm smile.

"Thanks, Daniel. I won't forget this."

"Well," he grinned playfully, "you've still gotta help me turn it into a home."

"No problemo," she replied, wiping her eyes.

Chapter 10

Maggie

Maggie sat back in her chair, twirling a pencil between her fingers, watching Daniel set up the map on the table. She loved Dungeons & Dragons nights—it was like stepping into another world. A world where she and Daniel could play out their fantasy personas without all the awkwardness that existed outside the game.

Daniel's voice broke through her thoughts. "Alright, everyone, tonight's quest is a dangerous one." He cleared his throat dramatically. "The party has been tasked with rescuing the villagers from a hobgoblin lair deep within the mountains. And," he smiled slightly, "you've been joined by a new ally: Sir Justin McWrath, Paladin of the Knights of the Black Cross. He wears a suit of adamantine armor, with a white surcoat bearing the black cross of his order. By his side is a long sword with a leather hilt and a gold filigree cross guard. He has dark hair cropped short, a bit of stubble and blazing blue eyes that almost seem to shine with a holy light."

"I introduce my character to him, bowing slightly," she said. "I am Aluria of the Selesian woods, druid of the order of the sun elves."

"He takes your hand, kisses the back of it, and in a husky voice, says 'Pleased to meet you, Milady. Your protector, always.'"

Her stomach flipped a little at the way Daniel introduced his character, Justin. She could picture him in her mind, tall and strong, his armor gleaming with the righteous fury of a protector. And of course, it was Daniel's voice that brought him to life, making it all the more fun.

The game was in full swing now, the group battling their way through the lair, spells flying, swords clashing. Maggie's druid, graceful and fierce, stood beside Justin as they faced down the hobgoblin chieftain in his cavern.

It was intense, everyone throwing dice and shouting out attacks. Daniel narrated the battle, his eyes gleaming with excitement as he described the blows raining down on their characters.

"The hobgoblin warlord Grognar swings," Daniel said. Then he rolled a die behind his screen. He gasped in a quick breath. "Ooh.."

"What happened?" Maggie asked.

"Critical hit," Daniel rolled some dice. "Yeah, this isn't good. Justin took a massive hit. Justin's barely holding on," he said. "He's down, but not out."

Maggie's heart pounded. Without thinking, she blurted out, "I run to his side and cast Cure Wounds."

Daniel's eyes met hers from across the table. "Are you sure?" he asked, his tone playful. "He still has healing points he can use on himself."

Maggie didn't miss a beat. "You're a friend, Justin," she said, her voice full of the druid's calm resolve. "Of course I'm going to save you." She rolled the dice, and her character knelt beside him, placing her hands on Justin's shoulder.

"I'm casting the spell," she added, and then, with a grin, she continued, "I lean down and kiss his forehead. 'It's the least I could do, brave and valiant knight,'" she said, her voice soft with mock affection.

The group chuckled, but it was Daniel's reaction she was focused on. His cheeks flushed slightly, and he shifted in his seat. "Justin... appreciates your gesture, but says, 'You didn't need to do that. I had points in my healing pool.'"

Maggie winked at him. "And I tell him, 'Too late, Paladin. You're already saved.'"

The group let out a few playful whistles, and Maggie smirked as Daniel ducked his head, trying to hide a smile. That was the first time she realized how fun this game could be—when it wasn't just the dice rolling that made her heart race.

The next game, a week later, felt like a continuation of their unspoken connection. This time, the stakes were higher. The party had traveled to Hawke's Reach, where the hobgoblin warlord had raised a massive army.

"The castle is being besieged on all fronts by the massive horde of goblins and hobgoblins under Grognar's remaining forces. This is the battle that will decide the fate of Hawke's Reach, the place you've been defending these past weeks," Daniel set up the board, including a brand-new castle diorama he'd built over the past few days in the back room of the shop. Maggie had asked what he was doing, but he shooed her away every time she tried to get a look at the massive two-foot square structure.

"You'll see it on Friday night," he said. She noticed him looking at her, into her eyes as he said it, and then looked away.

That night, the battle to defend the castle was fierce, and Maggie's druid was bloodied from the attacks, her health dropping dangerously low.

"I go down," Maggie said, her voice calm but knowing what was coming.

Daniel's voice was urgent as he narrated, "Grognar has you on the ground, raising his weapon, ready to deliver the final blow."

"On his initiative, Justin steps in." He paused, meeting Maggie's eyes. "He casts Lay on Hands and pulls Aluria to safety."

Maggie felt a shiver run down her spine at the way Daniel described it. "I hug Justin," she said, glancing at Daniel. "And I whisper in his ear, 'Thank you for saving me, but I could've healed myself.'"

Daniel coughed, clearly trying to stay in character. "Justin replies, 'My honor wouldn't allow you to do that while there are others to save.'"

Their friends made a few teasing comments, and Maggie tried not to smile too broadly. The tension was growing, and the more they played, the more these little moments seemed to blur the line between the game and reality.

The third game that month was the most intense. The battle was over, the toll of the dead counted. Maggie's druid had survived, thanks to Justin's protection. As the rest of the party settled into their camps for the night, Maggie decided to make her move.

"I go to Justin's camp," she announced, glancing around the table. The other players leaned forward, sensing where this was going.

Daniel looked up, a little surprised. "Alright. What do you do?"

Maggie grinned. "I enter his tent."

Daniel's eyes widened. "Okay... and?"

"I drop my leather corset," Maggie said, her voice calm but her heart racing. "And I start to take off my shirt."

Daniel's face flushed. "Wait, what are you doing?"

"I want to thank him," Maggie said with a sly smile. "For saving my life."

The other players started giggling and making playful comments. Maggie continued, "I crawl into bed with him and say, 'My love, I couldn't rest knowing I owed you my life. Let me return the favor.'"

Daniel coughed, visibly flustered. "Uh, we'll fade to black there," he said quickly, his cheeks bright red.

The table erupted in laughter and cheers. One of the players called out, "Oooohhh," while another clapped in approval.

Maggie leaned back in her chair, feeling her own face heat up, but the thrill of it was undeniable. She locked eyes with Daniel, and for a moment, neither of them said anything.

Then, slowly, a smile crept across his face.

That night, as they packed up the game, Maggie couldn't help but feel the shift between them. Something had changed—something deeper than the game, something real.

As Maggie walked out of the RV that night, she couldn't stop thinking about Daniel's reaction. The way he blushed, the way his eyes flickered with something more than just amusement. The line between Sir Justin McWrath and Daniel was blurring, and she wasn't sure if she was more excited or nervous to see where it might lead.

But one thing was clear—this was no longer just a game.

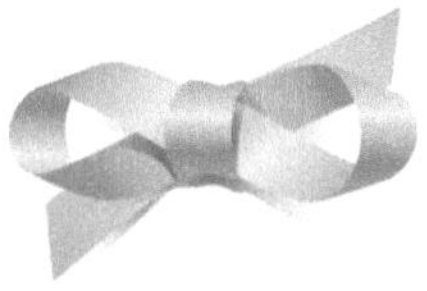

Chapter 11

Daniel

Over the next few days, Maggie and Daniel visited Bennet's Hardware, hoping the store would have everything they needed to fix up the loft. As they entered, the first person they noticed was a young blonde girl wearing a blue Bennet's apron, standing at the front with a big, welcoming smile.

"Lizzy!" Maggie exclaimed, rushing over to hug her friend. "Do you remember me from our D & D game last summer? How are you?"

Lizzy hugged her affectionately, grinning. "Maggie! Wow, I can't believe it's you!"

"That's right! How's my viral sensation?"

"I'm not sick," Lizzy said, looking confused.

Maggie laughed. "No, the video we made. Did your dad show you? When you played and killed the kobold king with Strawberry Girl the Barbarian?"

"Oh yeah!" Lizzy's face lit up with pride. "I took him down with my axe!"

"That's right. You're a total bad mama jama."

Lizzy beamed. "I'm a bad mama jama."

Just then, Derrick approached and extended his hand to Daniel. "How you doin', hoss? Maggie! Good to see you. Lizzie asks about you all the time." His broad smile matching the store manager name tag on his white shirt and tie.

"Well, look at you," Daniel said, shaking his hand and gesturing to the badge. "Movin' up in the world."

Derrick chuckled. "It's more of a joke, really. Jamie's dealing with some health issues, so I'm covering for him. I guess he figured I could handle it since I just got married and all."

"Congrats again. How's it going?"

Derrick smiled warmly. "It's going great. Never thought I'd fall so hard for anyone other than my little girl here." He ruffled Lizzy's hair, pulling her out of a deep conversation with Maggie about the next D&D game.

Daniel grinned. "New employee, huh?" he said, nodding toward Lizzy.

"Yeah, Jamie thought she'd make a good greeter. She's been doing great—customers love her."

"I'm sure they do," Daniel agreed.

Derrick shifted into business mode. "So, what can I get for you today?"

Daniel pulled a crumpled list from his pocket. "We're renovating the loft," he explained, glancing over at Maggie. "Got a new tenant."

Derrick raised an eyebrow, a smirk forming. "New tenant, huh? Good for you."

Daniel laughed. "Just get the stuff, would you?"

"Sure thing," Derrick teased. "Might take a week or two to get it all in, though. But we've got the basics like lumber, drywall, and toilets."

"That sounds perfect. And put it on my account—we're a little cash-strapped at the moment."

"You got it, brother," Derrick said. "I'll gather everything up. Do you want it delivered?"

"Yeah, anything I can't fit in the Acura. When can I get it?"

"In a couple of days."

"Perfect."

Two days later, the supplies arrived at the bookstore. Ralph and Rex, Bennet's delivery guys, helped Derrick move everything upstairs to the loft. Daniel signed off on the order, and he and Maggie got to work.

For the next few days, they worked tirelessly, putting together two-by-fours for the walls, nailing up drywall, and painting the space in a fresh off-white color. Daniel installed a brand-new water-saving toilet, reconnected the plumbing for the shower, replaced the shower-head, and installed a sleek new vanity and medicine cabinet.

Throughout the renovations, their banter was light and playful. Maggie joked about Daniel "giving her wood" while they hammered in the studs, and she teased him about putting fresh sheets on the temporary bed, suggesting he was welcome to sleep there any time.

By the end of the week, the once-dingy loft that had been cluttered with piles of books was transformed into a cozy, livable space. A new bed stood against the wall, paired with a crisp white couch from the local furniture store. The bathroom gleamed with sparkling silver and white fixtures, and the kitchen boasted a new sink, faucet, and refinished cabinets, completing the kitchenette's makeover.

"We make a great team," Maggie said, admiring their work. "Maybe we should audition for one of those renovation shows."

Daniel chuckled, glancing at her. "Yeah, we do, don't we?"

A slow, comfortable silence fell between them as they looked at each other. Daniel cleared his throat awkwardly. "Well, welcome home."

Maggie smiled and patted his arm. "Thanks, Danny Boy."

"Anytime, Magpie," he replied, slipping an arm around her. She leaned into his embrace, and for a moment, they simply stood there, taking in their shared accomplishment.

Chapter 12

Maggie

It was Thanksgiving. Maggie and Daniel pulled up in his Acura outside Rose's house. Maggie stepped out, carrying a bouquet of multi-colored flowers, while Daniel followed, holding a bottle of wine. Dressed in a sharp blue suit, Daniel looked dashing—Maggie had told him as much before they arrived. She wore a black blouse with long sleeves, covered by a delicate lace vest, and an orange flowing skirt that reached her ankles. Her black sandals clicked softly on the pavement as she moved, and her hair was braided and tied with an orange silk bow.

Daniel glanced at her, admiring her outfit—and, if he were honest with himself, her curvaceous figure. But he quickly shook the thought from his mind. Over the past few weeks, he had found himself looking at her like that more and more. She often exchanged knowing glances with him, too. It felt like they were caught in a dance, drawn closer by an invisible string that only tightened with time, edging them towards an inevitable kiss—and whatever might follow.

He knew it wasn't right. He was still mourning, and Maggie was eighteen years younger. She was only here temporarily, a friend of his daughter. The reasons not to pursue this were endless. Yet every time their eyes met, the longing and desire he felt became harder to resist.

They walked up to the white house nestled in the White Pines subdivision, where every home looked almost identical. Daniel glanced down the street at the row of similar houses and silently thanked the stars he still lived in the house where he and Cassandra had raised Rose, with neighbors not so close by.

Rose appeared at the door, and Daniel quickly removed his arm from Maggie's waist, hoping his daughter hadn't noticed. Rose greeted Maggie with a kiss on the cheek, then hugged her father.

"Thanks for coming. The turkey's almost ready," Rose said, turning to Maggie with a warm smile. "Good to see you again, Maggie. What brings you back to town?"

"I'm between jobs," Maggie replied. "I wanted to see family and friends before heading back west."

"Oh, you're still in L.A.?"

"Yeah. The gallery I was working for shut down after a disastrous showing. Apparently, papier-mâché elephants and gaudy sculptures of skyscraper-balancing elephants weren't as popular as we thought."

Rose laughed. "Not really my taste. How much were they asking for them?"

"Four to eight thousand apiece."

"Oof, no thanks."

"Yeah, that's what everyone else thought too," Maggie said with a shrug. "We sold maybe two pieces, both well below market price. After that, my boss couldn't keep the gallery running."

Rose chuckled. "I'm glad you're here, though. And with my dad, no less." She gave Daniel a playful look.

"Don't worry, darling," Daniel said with a light laugh as they entered the house. "Maggie's been working at the store, helping me clean up the place."

"That's nice," Rose said, glancing between them. "How's it going? Do you like working for my dad?"

Maggie grinned. "Oh, he's a real taskmaster."

Rose raised an eyebrow, noticing the shared smile between them. "Well, dinner's almost ready. Dave and the kids went to pick out a Christmas tree at the lot down the road. They should be back soon."

"Great," Daniel said. "I need to find the bathroom."

"It's down the hall, second door on the right. You've been here before, Dad."

Daniel chuckled. "It's been a while. I forget things."

As soon as he left, Rose turned to Maggie, her expression shifting. "Okay, so what's going on? What are you doing here?"

Maggie blinked, caught off guard. "Whoa, relax. I couldn't go to my parents' house dressed like this," she gestured to her outfit. "Daniel invited me. I hope that's okay? I can leave if it's a problem."

"No, no, it's fine," Rose said, her tone softening. "I'm happy to see you. It's just...a bit of a surprise, seeing you with my dad."

"Why would that be a surprise?" Maggie asked, raising an eyebrow.

Rose hesitated. "I remember how you used to talk about him when we were teenagers."

Maggie rolled her eyes. "That was a silly teenage crush."

Rose looked at her pointedly. "So, nothing's... happened between you two?"

Maggie flushed. "No. He wouldn't. Would he?"

"I certainly hope not," Rose replied firmly.

Maggie's mind raced. I certainly hope he does.

"Don't worry, Rose," Maggie said, regaining her composure. "We're just friends. I like your dad. He's given me a job, and he's a great guy. But he's grieving your mom, and let's be honest, he's old enough to be my dad."

"Good," Rose said, eyeing her closely. "Keep it that way."

"I will," Maggie said with a reassuring smile.

A honk outside interrupted their conversation. They peered out the window and saw Dave pulling into the driveway, a massive Christmas tree strapped to the roof of the minivan.

Daniel emerged from the bathroom just in time to see it. "I'll go help with that," he said, moving toward the door.

As Daniel joined Dave outside, Rose and Maggie resumed their conversation, the earlier tension fading. "So, how can I help with dinner?" Maggie asked.

"Cranberry sauce," Rose replied with a smile.

The two women moved around the kitchen in easy harmony, rekindling their old friendship as they prepared the Thanksgiving feast. By the time the turkey and all the fixings were on the table, the men had wrestled the Christmas tree inside and positioned it in the corner of the living room.

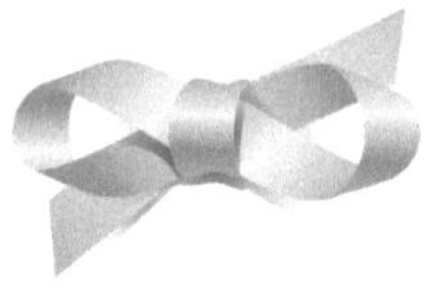

Chapter 13

Daniel

Throughout dinner, Daniel couldn't keep his eyes off Maggie. He participated in the conversation, chatting with Dave about his upcoming transition out of the service. Dave had been in the military for ten years and was ready to return to civilian life. He had been studying accounting in his free time—numbers had always come easily to him—and there was an opening at the local community college that a friend could help him secure.

Meanwhile, Rose and the kids were laughing about the next Pokémon they planned to catch in Pokémon Go, a game Daniel admitted he didn't understand.

"Maggie here set up Excel for me," Daniel added, looking at her warmly. "She's been handling the bookkeeping too."

"Dad," Rose said with a light chuckle, "I told you Dave could've done that."

"You refused to take any money from me," Daniel replied. "And I want to pay someone for their work. It's the right thing to do, son."

Dave shrugged. "Your call."

"Besides," Daniel said, turning back to Maggie, "she's been doing a great job." He winked at her, and Maggie blushed. Rose noticed.

"So, what else do you do at the store?" Rose asked pointedly.

Maggie smiled. "I'm reorganizing the shelves, updating the signs so people can actually read them. Your dad's handwriting is... let's just say, unique. Sometimes, I can't tell if he's writing 'fiction' or 'function.'"

Daniel laughed. "It's fiction."

Maggie smirked. "Well, sometimes it's hard to tell."

"It's a bookstore. Of course, it's fiction," Daniel said, his eyes locked on hers. For a moment, it felt like the rest of the dinner guests had disappeared, leaving only the two of them in conversation.

"Maybe write it in block letters instead of cursive?"

"That's how I write, if you can't read it then learn to write that way."

"Oh, I know how to write cursive, I don't know what the heck that chicken scratch is." Daniel and Maggie both seemed to enjoy this back-and-forth banter. He looked over at his daughter.

"Chicken scratch, she says," he said.

Rose interrupted the growing tension. "Anyone want pumpkin pie?"

Maggie shook her head. "Oh no, I'm stuffed. Besides, I have to keep my figure in check." She patted her stomach playfully.

Daniel looked at her with affection. "Your figure is perfect, hon. Don't worry about that."

Rose coughed abruptly. "Dad," she said, standing up. "I need your help with something out back."

Daniel blinked, a little confused. "Can't Dave help you?"

"No, it's a Christmas decoration. I need your opinion on something."

"Can it wait?" he asked, glancing at the half-finished desserts on the table. "We're about to have dessert."

"Dave can help the kids," Rose insisted.

"Okay," Daniel said, standing up and looking around the table. "Let's go see what this is all about."

They walked out the back door, and as soon as they were outside, Rose lit a cigarette, turning to face him with a serious expression.

"What the hell was that?" she asked, jabbing a finger back toward the house.

"What do you mean?"

"That," Rose snapped. "That... flirting."

"Flirting?" Daniel blinked. "I don't know what you're talking about."

"You don't know?" Rose took a deep drag from her cigarette. "You haven't noticed how she's been looking at you all night?"

"Who?" Daniel asked, feigning innocence. "Maggie?"

"Yes, Maggie! Who else would I be talking about?"

Daniel sighed. "Come on, honey. It's not like that."

"Oh, it's not?" Rose raised an eyebrow. "Because I watched her practically eye-fuck you the entire dinner."

"Eye-fuck?" Daniel's brow furrowed in confusion. "What does that even mean?"

Rose took another drag, visibly frustrated. "Every time you look at her, she's looking right back at you. What's going on between you two?"

Daniel stepped closer to his daughter, gently placing his hands on her arms. "Honey, listen to me. There's nothing going on. If there's any flirting, it's just harmless banter. She's too young, I'm still grieving your mother, and Maggie is only here for a few months. She's your best friend from school. You really think I would cross that line?"

Rose stared at him, her cigarette dangling between her fingers. "So, it's just friendly banter? Nothing more?"

"Just friends," Daniel assured her. "That's all it is. Don't worry."

Rose exhaled slowly, nodding. "Okay. It's just... you know how it looks."

"I know," Daniel replied gently. "But how things look and what's actually happening aren't always the same. We've talked about it. Maggie and I both agreed—nothing's going to happen."

"Good." Rose took a final puff of her cigarette, dropping it and crushing it underfoot. "But I did actually need your opinion on the Christmas decorations."

She led him around to the front yard, where an inflatable Grinch and a Buddy the Elf figure lay tangled on the lawn, courtesy of Dave's hasty attic retrieval.

"So," Rose said, crossing her arms, "which one do we go with this year? Dave wants Buddy, but I'm leaning toward the Grinch. The kids don't care either way."

Daniel chuckled softly, gazing at the figures. "Go with Buddy. It was your mom's favorite."

Rose smiled, her face softening. "I miss her most this time of year."

Daniel pulled her into a hug. "I miss her too, sweetie," he said quietly. "I miss her every day."

As Daniel pulled up to Maggie's apartment, the car idled for a moment longer than it should have. They both stayed seated, neither one eager to leave, tension crackling in the air between them. Maggie, flushed from that extra glass of wine at dinner, glanced over at him, her lips slightly parted as if searching for something to say. He caught that glimpse, her lips glistening, and for a heartbeat, it was the most divine thing he'd seen in years.

"I had a really good time," Daniel said softly, turning towards her, his voice filled with a warmth that lingered.

"Me too," Maggie replied, her eyes catching his. "Thanks for having me."

They had been flirting all night—stealing glances, brushing hands as they worked together to set up Dave's Christmas tree, their fingers touching briefly as they handed each other ornaments. When she stood beside him, admiring the final decorations, her arm had snaked behind his back, and the way the tree lights twinkled in her eyes had taken him somewhere he hadn't been in a long time.

"Maggie..." he started, his voice barely more than a whisper.

She tilted her head, waiting, hopeful.

Daniel reached over, hesitating for just a breath, and then she met him halfway. Their lips touched, tentative, like a bee testing a flower. The kiss was brief, but before either could pull away, he reached behind her neck, pulling her in closer. Their lips met again, this time more urgently, and when their tongues touched, it felt like the dam of restraint he'd built had finally burst. He deepened the kiss, tasting her, feeling her warmth, and for several long, intoxicating moments, Daniel forgot everything but her.

When he finally pulled back, breathless, there was a silence—thick, heavy with the weight of everything that hadn't been said.

"Maggie, I..." He stopped, the words tangled in his throat.

She motioned toward the apartment. "We don't have to end the evening now."

Daniel sighed deeply. "No... I have a lot to think about, and this... it wouldn't be right."

Maggie lowered her gaze. "I understand. I'm sorry, I didn't mean to—"

"No, it's me," he interrupted, his tone gentle but firm. "That kiss... it was good. Real good. The first one I've had in five years."

She smiled softly. "Did you like it? As much as I did?"

Daniel chuckled. "More than I should, and that's the problem."

"Why is that a problem?" she asked, her tone playful, teasing him.

"I can't answer that right now," Daniel admitted, staring at the steering wheel for a moment. "Because if I'm being honest, I don't see it as a problem... and that's a problem."

"I see," Maggie said, her eyes gleaming with mischief. She leaned over, planting a soft kiss on his cheek. "Thanks for a lovely evening, Daniel."

He caught her before she could fully pull away. "Magpie..."

She turned back, and this time, Daniel held her face gently in his hands, his lips finding hers once more. This kiss was longer, deeper, filled with the unspoken longing that had lingered between them all evening. When they finally broke apart, Maggie's eyes fluttered open, her breath unsteady.

"Wow," she murmured, a smile creeping across her lips. "That felt... good."

Daniel nodded slowly. "Yeah... and that's what worries me."

She raised an eyebrow. "So, you wanna come up?"

He chuckled, shaking his head. "No, I don't do that on the first date."

Maggie grinned. "Technically, this is our second."

"Let's say third, then."

"Okay, Danny boy," she said, laughing. "I'll hold you to it."

"Don't get your hopes up," he teased. "I might change my mind."

"I'll try." Maggie winked, and for a moment, they were just two people playing a familiar game.

"In the meantime, take the rest of the weekend off. I'll see you Monday," Daniel sat back in his seat, wondering if he should accept her invitation.

"Maybe before?"

"No," Daniel said, suddenly serious. "I need time to think."

She smiled, turning to leave. "I know where you live, remember?"

Daniel smirked. "Yes, I do. But try to forget for the next few days."

"I'll try, but I can't make any promises." She gave him a playful wave and started to step out of the car.

"Maggie," Daniel called, his voice stopping her. "Really... I need to think about things."

Maggie leaned against the door, her expression softening. "Don't think too long, Daniel. I leave in January, remember?"

Daniel's heart skipped a beat. "Don't worry... it won't take that long."

She smiled at him, a knowing look in her eyes. "See that it doesn't."

"I like you, Maggie," he said. "A lot. And that's what scares me."

"Good," she said. "I'm glad we had this chat. See you Monday, Danny boy."

"See you Monday, Magpie."

He watched her walk away, wondering what he was doing, why he was doing it, and admiring the way the orange skirt fluttered around her legs and ass. A million synapses told him to go after her. But he started the Acura and drove away, wondering if he could stop thinking about her lips on his.

Chapter 14

Daniel

It was a gray, overcast December day that matched Daniel's mood. He and Bill sat at the small table near the front of the bookstore, a chessboard between them. The shop had just opened, and there weren't any customers yet. The soft sound of the pieces being moved echoed in the quiet room.

Daniel made his move, capturing one of Bill's knights. "So," Daniel said, "have you talked to that girl at La Perk yet?"

Bill sighed, shaking his head. "I send her flowers every week. Isn't that enough?"

"You've got to stop sending her flowers and just give them to her in person," Daniel said, moving his bishop across the board.

"Have you looked at me?" Bill gestured to his round stomach and the thinning hair on his head. "I'm overweight, partially bald, and old. Did I mention I'm fat?"

Daniel chuckled. "Yeah, but I'm sure she'll see right through that to the real you. You're rich, Bill. That's got to count for something."

Bill snorted. "Sure, because women are only interested in money."

They moved a couple more pieces, the game easily continuing as they bantered back and forth. The bell above the door jingled, and they both looked up. A man strolled in—tall, about six-foot-two, with dark, wavy hair and a neatly trimmed black beard. He was dressed in a sharp gray suit with a black tie, exuding an air of self-importance.

"How do you do, gentlemen?" the man said with a smile that didn't reach his eyes.

Daniel stood up, eyeing the newcomer. "Can I help you?"

The man extended his hand. "Ellis Marleigh. I'm here to talk about the rent."

Daniel frowned, shaking his hand reluctantly. "But I paid it this month. Where's Jake?"

Ellis's smile grew wider, but there was no warmth in it. "My father had a stroke. He's in a coma and not expected to make it to the end of the year. Tragic, really."

Daniel blinked, taken aback by the nonchalant way Ellis delivered the news. "I'm sorry to hear that."

"Thank you," Ellis said, though the crocodile tears in his tone didn't match the words. "Anyway, I'm handling his affairs now, which brings me to your rent."

Daniel crossed his arms. "Jake gave me a grace period and kept it low because of my wife's passing."

"Oh?" Ellis tilted his head, feigning interest. "When did she pass?"

"Five years ago," Daniel said quietly.

Ellis clapped his hands together, the sound echoing in the empty store. "So, you've been coasting on my father's sympathy for five years, huh? Got it. Well, that's over now. In January, the rent goes up."

Daniel's brow furrowed. "How much are we talking?"

Ellis tapped his chin as if calculating something in his head. "Well, adjusting for inflation, property taxes, upkeep... let's see... Oh, yes, there were renovations to the windows five years ago."

Daniel bristled. "That was because some kids threw a brick through it. Insurance should've covered it."

"Funny you should mention that. Insurance rates went up because of the incident." Ellis's voice was syrupy sweet as he continued. "So, all things considered, the new rent is going to be $1,750 a month, starting in January. Paid in full on the 1st of every month, but I'm a nice guy, so I'll give you a few extra days since it's the new year. See how good I am?"

"That's over a thousand dollars more," Daniel said, his voice strained.

Ellis shrugged. "Yes, it is. But surely books have gone up in price in the last ten years, right?" He gestured around the store. "Looks like you've got plenty of inventory. Maybe have a sale or something."

Bill pointed to a sign above Ellis's head that read, "Used Books 25% Off."

Ellis glanced up at the sign, smirking. "Well, there you go. I'm sure the customers are rolling in." He inched the bridge of his nose and continued. "And what's that smell?"

Daniel felt his jaw tighten, his fists clenching at his sides. Before he could respond, Maggie stepped out from the back room, having overheard the conversation. "That smell you're commenting on? That's the old book smell. People come in just for that."

Ellis turned to her, flashing his teeth in another insincere smile. "Well, if only people could pay for a smell, huh?" He looked back at Daniel. "So, what I'm hearing is you're not selling anything but a whiff of dirt and used books nobody wants at a discount. Good luck getting that rent." He pulled a business card from his pocket, handing it to Maggie. "If you don't pay, eviction follows. That should give you some incentive, don't you think?"

Daniel stared at him, speechless. "You can't do this. It's part of the lease."

Ellis raised an eyebrow. "You're welcome to call Jake. I'm sure it'll be a riveting conversation, seeing as how he's in a coma." He winked, making finger guns at Daniel. "You're dealing with me now, and the price is final. Any questions? Call me." He gave a mock salute and turned to leave.

As the door swung shut, Daniel stood frozen, his anger boiling under the surface. Bill glanced at him. "Is there anything you can do? Don't you have people in the government you could call?"

Bill shook his head slowly. "This is standard practice, Daniel. I'm not sure what we can do. Maybe a flash sale?"

"I'll figure something out." Daniel sighed, his mind racing. "We could dress up like three ghosts and make his Christmas Eve a living hell, like Dickens did with Ebenezer."

"No," Bill leaned forward, lowering his voice. "Don't do that. You'll regret it."

Maggie, who had been quiet until now, looked between the two men. "Ebenezer?"

Bill explained. "Scrooge...from A Christmas Carol. It was an anniversary gift for Cassie, a first edition signed copy of her favorite book. It's worth a lot now—Daniel found it at an auction, paid a pretty penny for it."

Daniel said, "It was in a private collection, so it's near mint. Probably could get ten, twelve thousand for it."

Maggie shook her head. "Don't sell it, Daniel. There has to be another way."

Daniel rubbed his face, feeling the weight of it all pressing down on him. "It's the only way I can see right now. I've got a buyer in Raleigh. I could make the call."

Maggie stepped closer; her voice soft but firm. "Let me talk to my dad. Maybe he can help."

Daniel stiffened. "I'm not a charity case. I can handle this. Don't worry about it."

"Okay. I trust you." She gave him a small, encouraging smile before walking back to the stockroom, Ellis's card still in her pocket. "Just think about it, please?"

"I will," he said, looking at the glass case behind him that held his more precious volumes. He saw the leather spline, and the embossed gold words, beckoning like currency. This was going to be a hard decision. Sell his most treasured book in his collection? Or close the store for good.

Chapter 15

Maggie

She couldn't stop thinking about that kiss. That scorching Thanksgiving kiss. Who had started it? Him, her, or both? Or maybe it was the wine. They hadn't talked about it all weekend, and now it was Monday. The shop had been busy nonstop. There were customers, sales, and errands—especially with Black Friday breaking sales records. But now, they finally had a moment to sit down, just the two of them, over a quiet lunch in the back room.

Daniel pulled a package of lunch meat from the refrigerator, laying it on the table, followed by a block of cheese. He was making a sandwich, seemingly focused on the task, when Maggie slipped up behind him. She wrapped her arms around his waist, feeling the warmth of his body through his sweater.

"Okay," she said softly, her lips close to his ear. "You're either avoiding me, or you hate me, or... you want to kiss me like you did three nights ago and can't decide which you want more."

He stiffened slightly, but she could feel the tension wasn't from discomfort. "What do you mean?" he asked, voice low.

Maggie stepped back just enough to look at him. "We had that great time on Thanksgiving, and then that kiss... And now, it feels like you've been avoiding me."

"I'm not avoiding you," he said, turning toward her. His eyes softened as he touched her chin gently, lifting her face so their eyes met. "I think I've been avoiding myself."

Her breath hitched at the touch, heat rising in her cheeks. "Don't change the subject," she said, though the softness in his touch made her melt inside. She wanted to hold onto her frustration, but the way he looked at her...

"The kiss?" she asked, her voice barely above a whisper.

"Yes, the kiss." His eyes lingered on her lips. "I liked it."

"So did I."

"I want more," he admitted. And before she could respond, his lips were on hers.

The kiss deepened quickly, hunger and longing pouring into it. Maggie's arms tightened around his waist, pulling him closer, her body responding instantly to the feel of him. His hands moved up to cup her face, fingers threading through her hair as the kiss grew more intense.

Her knees weakened as his touch trailed down her neck, over her shoulders, and toward the strap of her black dress. She widened her stance, his knee pressing into her, opening her up even more. She couldn't get enough of him, the heat between them nearly unbearable as their breaths came fast and shallow.

Then, from the front of the store, the distant chime of the bell rang.

"Shit," they both whispered, pulling apart with a mixture of frustration and amusement.

"More later?" Daniel asked, brushing a stray lock of hair from her face.

"Definitely more," she said, trying to catch her breath.

They composed themselves quickly before heading out to the front room, where a man stood chatting with Bill.

"Hey, Daniel," the man greeted, his voice jovial. He wore jeans and a rugged leather jacket, reminiscent of an Indiana Jones film. "I wasn't expecting you until after lunch."

Daniel forced a smile, though Maggie could see the reluctance behind it. "Gerald, hey. You're early."

"When you're about to buy a rare treasure, you don't wait," Gerald said with a grin.

"I get it," Daniel said, shaking his hand. "I really hate to let her go, but... when needs must, right?"

"Right." Gerald smiled again.

Turning to Maggie, Daniel introduced them. "Maggie, this is Gerald Henson, an old friend from Raleigh."

"Pleased to meet you," Maggie said, though her attention quickly turned to Daniel. "What's the treasure?"

"A Christmas Carol," Daniel said, his voice tinged with regret. "I decided to sell it to my best friend here."

Gerald chuckled. "Best rival, more like."

Daniel smiled at the banter, but it was clear there was a heavyweight behind this sale. He walked over to the locked display cabinet, took out a key, and carefully removed the book. "Here she is," he said, handing it over to Gerald, who donned nylon gloves before taking it.

Gerald's eyes widened as he carefully opened the book. "Signed by the man himself. First printing... This is incredible."

"How did you keep it so pristine?" Gerald asked, marveling at the condition.

Daniel shrugged. "Comic book bags help. And it's been behind glass since... well, since forever." His voice trailed off, a somber note hanging between the words.

Gerald patted Daniel's shoulder gently. "I know this is hard for you."

Daniel nodded, his expression hard to read. "Just... keep it safe, okay?"

"You have my word," Gerald said sincerely.

As they discussed the sale, Maggie watched, a spark of an idea forming in her mind. When the time came for goodbyes, she approached Gerald. "Could I get your business card? Just in case I'm ever in Raleigh."

"Of course." Gerald handed her a card with a smile.

Maggie tucked it into her pocket as the two men shook hands. As Gerald left, Daniel lingered for a moment, his eyes still on the door. Maggie glanced at him, wishing he didn't have to do that, wishing they could go to the back room and kiss more. Then an idea formed, and she smiled. I know where you live, mister book seller man.

Chapter 16

Maggie

Maggie coasted into the driveway of Daniel's two-story home, the same one where she'd first met him all those years ago. She remembered sitting on the couch, watching a movie about a Black sheriff and the town of Rock Ridge. She didn't want him to hear her approach. It was late, the moon hung in a half-light, and the house was dark except for a faint glow from the kitchen window.

"I can't believe I'm doing this," she muttered, tugging down her miniskirt.

The tall wooden fence surrounding the house loomed ahead, with the gate leading to the backyard just where she remembered. The layout of the house was still fresh in her mind, from those times spent there with her friend Rose. She knew the master bedroom was on the first floor, and she'd noticed recently that Daniel still used it, making her plan even easier to pull off.

As she slipped through the gate as quietly as possible, it gave a faint creak. She froze. *God, I hope he's not awake.*

She crept around the house, past the bushes lining the walls, until she reached the deck that wrapped around the back. She took off her shoes, going barefoot to the window she knew led to his bedroom.

It's now or never, she thought. *I can't believe I'm doing this.*

The idea had come to her a few days ago, and she'd spent the time since perfecting her plan.

Will he think this is sexy or just... crazy? she wondered. *What's the worst that could happen? Kick me out of the loft? Fire me?*

Knowing Daniel, he probably wouldn't do any of those things. But he would likely be stern with her and set some boundaries.

Why does this guy have to be so good?

She found the window and tried to lift it. It didn't budge. Damn. She knocked lightly at first, waiting a few seconds before knocking again. A light flicked on inside.

"Daniel?" she whispered, unsure if her voice carried through the glass.

More movement came from inside. The latch turned, and through the blinds, she saw him peek out, his hair tousled and eyes bleary.

"Magpie?" he mumbled, confused. "What the—?"

She waved with a sheepish smile.

He shoved his hair back from his face and blinked at her. "What are you doing here?"

"I thought I'd surprise you. It's cold. Can I come in?"

"Is everything okay? Why didn't you just use the front door?"

"Daniel, can you open the window and let me explain?"

He shook his head, still half-asleep, but unlocked the window and opened it, letting the cool night air into the room. She climbed in, landing on the bed—exactly where she wanted to be. He steadied her, helping her catch her breath.

"Well, this is a surprise."

"It is, isn't it?" She laughed. "How are you?"

"I was asleep. Am I dreaming this?"

"Nope, it's me." She reached out, touching his arm. He flinched slightly, still processing the situation.

"What are you doing here?" he asked again, more awake now.

"I wanted to surprise you. Do something... sexy."

He glanced at her outfit—a thin halter top, tight miniskirt, and nothing else. "Well, it's definitely a surprise... and sexy."

She grinned, leaning in to kiss him. "Now," she whispered, "no more talking."

"Maggie, I don't know if—"

She kissed him again, her arms wrapping around his neck as she tugged at his shirt.

"Wait, Mags—"

"Stop talking," she insisted, her breath warm against his skin. "I want you, Daniel."

"I want you too, but... I don't know about this."

"I do," she whispered, trailing kisses down his chest, her fingers toying with the hem of his shirt.

He laid back, torn between hesitation and desire, as she teased him, her touch igniting the tension between them.

"Tell me you want me," she murmured against his lips. "Tell me I'm yours."

"I want you," he breathed, but his hands found her shoulders, gently pushing her back. "But I want to do this first."

With a playful smirk, he lifted her halter top, revealing her bare skin beneath. He kissed her breasts, his hands caressing her softly. She arched into his touch, the sensations stirring something deep within her.

He kissed his way down her stomach, pausing as he tugged at her skirt. He glanced up and grinned. "Nothing underneath?"

"I knew what I was doing," she said, her voice hitching as his tongue found her inner thigh.

"You're beautiful," he murmured, kissing her gently before his tongue flicked over her clit. She gasped, her body responding instinctively, hips lifting to meet his mouth.

As he explored her with his tongue, his fingers joined, slipping inside her. Her body tensed at his touch, pleasure building with each movement.

"Daniel," she moaned, gripping the sheets, her thighs trembling around his head as he brought her closer to the edge. "Right there. Don't stop."

His fingers pressed deeper; his tongue relentless. She could feel the heat building, the pleasure cresting like a wave about to break. Her body tightened, then exploded into release.

"That's it, baby," he whispered against her skin, his fingers slowing as she trembled beneath him. "That's good. You taste so good."

She lay there, breathless. "Jesus Christ," she panted. "That was... incredible."

"I can do it again if you want," he teased.

She laughed softly, her hand resting on his chest. "No, I want to... return the favor."

He pulled her into his arms. "Let's just hold each other first."

She nestled against him, content, but as she reached for him, stroking his length, she noticed something was off. His body wasn't responding.

"Hey, you okay?" she asked, her voice soft.

He hesitated. "Yeah... I just..."

"It's fine," she said gently, smiling at him. "You're tired. Or maybe it's something else?"

"Something else," he admitted with a note of frustration.

She kissed his shoulder, wrapping her arms around him. "Don't feel bad."

"I want to be your lover," he said, kissing her forehead. "I really do. This just caught me off guard."

"I get it," she said, placing a finger to his lips. "Let's just lie here. Touch each other. Maybe sleep."

He pulled her close. "You want to sleep with me?"

"I do."

She rested her head on his chest, the sound of his heartbeat calming her as they drifted off together. His soft snores eventually filled the quiet room, making her smile. She waited a while before slipping out of bed, silently crawling back through the window and returning to the loft.

Chapter 17

Daniel

He moved his king's pawn to capture Bill's knight. "I think I have a problem with Maggie."

"Doesn't seem like a problem," Bill replied, moving his rook to take the pawn.

"Why do you say that?"

"Well," Bill said, "she's into you. Obviously."

"I know," Daniel muttered, moving his knight to the center of the board. "That's the problem."

"Why?"

"Because," Daniel said, as if that explained everything.

Bill sighed, moving his queen out. "Danny, do you know how lucky you are?"

"Don't call me Danny. You know how I hate it." Bill had taken to calling him "Danny" only when he wanted to drive a point home. And every time, Daniel knew Bill was right on some level. They'd known each other since they were fourteen. They shared the same birthday—though Daniel was born in Detroit and Bill in San Diego. Technically, Bill was older, but if you factored in the time zone difference, Daniel liked to joke that he was older. It was a source of their friendly banter.

"Okay, I won't call you Danny," Bill said with a smirk. "But you'll see I'm right."

"How lucky am I?" Daniel asked, leaning back.

"You've got a nice woman who likes you and wants to spend time with you. Don't think I haven't seen how you two look at each other. She's always giving you those moony eyes, and you do the same right back. And after Thanksgiving? It's gotten worse. It's almost sickening. I'm jealous."

"You could have one of your own, you know."

"Don't change the subject."

"All you need to do is tell Charlotte you've been sending the roses. Voilà, instant date."

"Don't bring me into this," Bill said, waving it off. "We're talking about your love life, not mine." Bill moved his queen to threaten Daniel's king.

"Well, I wouldn't call it a love life," Daniel admitted, shifting uncomfortably. "We've kissed a few times. And last night... well, I don't even know what that was."

"What happened last night?" Bill raised an eyebrow. "You want to pay attention to the game, Danny boy?"

But Daniel couldn't focus on the game. His mind kept drifting back to Maggie crawling through his bedroom window and their heated moment that never quite reached its conclusion.

"She snuck into my bedroom window last night."

Bill's eyes widened. "She what?"

"Yeah. I told her she could have knocked, but she said this way was more fun."

"And what did you do?"

Daniel rubbed the back of his neck. "We talked... made out a little. We almost went all the way, but I got cold feet and couldn't do it."

"Cold feet?" Bill asked, raising an eyebrow. "Or cold something else?"

Daniel ignored the jab, moving his king out of check. "My head wasn't in it."

"You're an idiot," Bill said, shaking his head. "What's your problem?"

"My problem is, she's too young, she's my daughter's friend, and my wife—who I loved for twenty-five years—died five years ago and still haunts me every time I think about anything romantic."

Bill leaned back in his chair, folding his arms. "Let me tell you something about that."

"Go ahead."

"Your wife is dead. You've got a woman who wants you. Take it. You've got an opportunity here. Seize the day. Carpe that fucking diem."

Daniel sighed deeply. "So, you're saying I should go for it?"

"Yes!" Bill threw his hands up in exasperation. "Didn't you tell me she's leaving in January?"

"Yeah. I did. So why start something if she's going to be gone in a couple of months?"

"Have a fling," Bill said simply. "Get back on the horse. Then, when she's gone, you'll be ready to date again. You can see where things go from there."

"So... you're saying I should start dating again?"

"That's exactly what I'm saying." Bill demanded. "It's what I've been saying for three years."

"And what about Cassandra?" Daniel's voice softened. "How could I look at her picture, knowing she's watching me from wherever she is?"

Bill's expression turned serious. "Listen, I knew her as well as you did. We were all friends. She loved you, man. And she would understand. Trust me."

"You sure?"

"Yes, I'm sure." Bill moved his queen into position, and Daniel realized it was a checkmate. "She'd want you to be happy."

Daniel sighed, feeling the weight of the conversation. "If something happens, I'll seriously consider it."

Bill shook his head, grinning. "It's like talking to a brick wall with you sometimes."

"I hear what you're saying. I just... I need to talk to her first. Figure out what happens next."

"I know what happens next," Bill said, smirking. "You mount the woman."

Daniel rolled his eyes, picking up the chess pieces to reset the board. "Crude, Bill."

"Accurate," Bill countered. "And judging by that smile, you know I'm right."

Daniel chuckled. "Okay, I'll talk to her. If it happens, it happens."

"Attaboy." Bill leaned back in his chair, satisfied. "She's got some boxes of books coming next week, right? You can talk to her when you help her move into the loft."

"You want to help?" Daniel asked.

"And be a third wheel while you grunt and struggle up the steps trying to be all manly? Absolutely not."

"Coward," Daniel said, shaking his head.

"Being a friend," Bill corrected. "Now move."

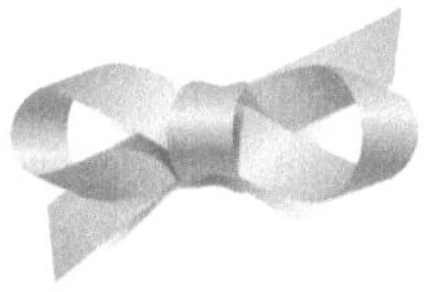

Chapter 18

Daniel

Daniel huffed up the stairs, carrying yet another heavy box of books. This one felt heavier than the others, and earlier, he'd spent hours assembling an IKEA bookshelf to store them. Reaching the top of the stairs, he let out a sigh of relief. "Finally," he muttered.

Maggie, lounging on the bed and sorting through her books, grinned. "Look at my big, strong, handsome hero," she teased.

He chuckled, watching her as she eyed the newly assembled bookshelf. She shook her head. "I think I'm going to need another one soon."

Daniel raised an eyebrow. "Another one? Just how long were you planning on staying?" he asked with a smirk.

Maggie walked over, kissed him on the cheek, and said, "Maybe longer than I thought."

"I thought you were only staying until January," he said, trying to keep things light.

"I don't know yet, Danny boy. How about we figure it out as we go?" she replied.

"Okay," he mused, rubbing the back of his neck. "I can do that."

"Good," she smiled. "Now, about that other bookshelf..."

"Guess we're going shopping again," he sighed.

"Yay!" She clapped her hands excitedly.

"Must be nice having a sugar daddy," he joked, plopping down on the bed.

Maggie laughed. "Oh, don't worry. You'll get paid back soon; you'll see."

"You know I'm not looking for that," Daniel said, leaning back.

"I know," she said softly, sitting next to him. "But you've been so kind to me. I want to give you something in return."

"All in good time," he replied, stretching his arms. "I'm tuckered out."

Maggie rubbed his back gently, then kissed his cheek again.

Daniel glanced at her, a mischievous glint in his eye. "You keep doing that, and we'll never go shopping."

"That's the idea," she said, her voice playful.

He grinned but then looked toward the window. "We've got that storm coming, and I'd like to get everything done before the snow gets worse."

"Don't worry," Maggie said, waving it off. "It's just a light dusting. The weatherman said an inch or two—nothing major."

"I hope you're right," Daniel said, a little concerned. "I'm supposed to be at Rose's place tomorrow to spend Christmas Eve."

Maggie pouted dramatically. "Aww, you don't want to spend Christmas with me? I'm hurt!"

He laughed, shaking his head. "It's not that. I just promised her I'd be there." After a moment's pause, an idea struck him. "Hey, why don't you come with me?"

Maggie hesitated; her expression thoughtful. "I don't know. I feel like I'd be intruding... And well, we haven't exactly introduced ourselves as a couple to her yet. Thanksgiving was awkward enough. I had to stretch the truth when Rose asked about us."

"Yeah, that was a bit uncomfortable," Daniel admitted. He stood and stretched. "Alright, let's make a plan. We'll go shopping, grab some dinner, and then get to work on these boxes. How about chicken parm?"

Maggie's face lit up. "That sounds perfect. Let's go!"

Chapter 19

Maggie

She sat on the edge of the couch, watching the news as the weatherman spoke in a serious tone. "This once-in-a-lifetime snowstorm hitting the Southeast hasn't happened around Christmas time in thirty-five years." Outside the window, snow had already begun piling up, swirling in thick, heavy flurries.

Daniel emerged from the bathroom, wiping his hands on a towel, his face flushed from the effort of carrying up several boxes of books she'd had shipped from her apartment in LA. He glanced at the boxes stacked against the wall and asked, "Why did you send these here if you're leaving on the first?"

Maggie shrugged, smiling softly. "I like to have my books with me. It's easier this way, and I need something to do. If I don't want to keep them, I can always donate them to you."

Daniel chuckled. "With all the books I already have in the basement, I don't think I need more."

She watched him, noticing the way his forearms flexed as he rubbed his hands together for warmth. His biceps were tight, his skin still glistening slightly from the exertion of lifting the heavy boxes. The sight of him made her pulse quicken.

"You know," she said, her voice playful, "You could stay. It's freezing out there, and the storm's only getting worse."

Daniel shook his head, sighing as he glanced toward the door. "No, I can't. My daughter will be worried. I was supposed to spend the night with her for Christmas tomorrow."

Maggie turned her gaze back to the TV, where the newscaster was warning of treacherous road conditions. "The roads are dangerous. The guy just said it."

"What guy?" Daniel asked, raising an eyebrow.

She gestured to the TV. "The guy on the news. And besides, it's warm here, and your fingers feel like ice." She grabbed his hands, holding them between hers, trying to transfer some warmth.

"Yeah, well, I just washed them," he said with a grin, squeezing her hands back gently. His eyes met hers, and for a moment, they stood there, locked in the quiet tension between them. His eyes always reminded her of starlight—calm, steady, and just out of reach.

"Do you really have to go?" she asked, her voice soft.

"I do," Daniel said, though there was a flicker of hesitation in his eyes.

"Maybe you can stay for a celebratory drink," she offered, pulling a bottle from the small rack by the kitchen counter.

He hesitated, looking from the bottle to her. "Well... maybe just a little. What is it?"

She grinned. "It's a twenty-year-old wheat ale, brewed by a sect of Carolingian monks in Belgium. They make a new batch every year, only about 4,000 bottles. It's amazing. You've got to try it."

He took a sip and blinked in surprise. "Wow, what's in this?"

"Only 18% alcohol," she said with a teasing smile.

Daniel sat down on the couch, running his hand over his face. "I feel like my head is already buzzing from that one gulp." He leaned back, staring at the bottle. "But I really have to go..."

Maggie moved closer, watching him. "Are you sure? You can even make it to your car?" She glanced out the window. The snow was coming down harder now, coating everything in a thick, white blanket.

Daniel stood, looking out at the storm. "I need to get going. Rose is expecting me. And what would Bill think if he saw me coming down from your loft in the morning?"

Maggie smirked. "He'd probably laugh and pat you on the back."

Daniel chuckled softly but didn't move. "She was hoping I'd be there to help with the kids and the unwrapping in the morning."

"Then call her. Let her know you're snowed in." She gently tugged at his coat, slipping it off his shoulders. Their eyes met again, the air between them growing heavier, charged. She looked at the gray stubble of his hair, noticing he'd just had it cut. He looked handsome in the low light of the loft candles.

"Maybe I should call an Uber," he said. "I'm sure there's one or more fools out there tonight."

"If you can't get out, what makes you think they can?"

"Maggie, I really have to go," he said. He started to pull away, but she noticed it was halfhearted. "You know, it's almost like you put a spell on me."

"Maybe I did," she grinned. He looked at her, the tension building as her hand brushed his cheek, soft and deliberate. "Do you really need this coat?" she asked in a whisper.

"No," Daniel murmured, shaking his head as his resolve crumbled. "I guess not."

Their lips met in a soft, lingering kiss; the kind that made everything else melt away. Daniel broke away for a moment, glancing out the window at the swirling blizzard. He let out a sigh and pulled out his phone. "Give me a minute. I'll let her know."

Maggie smiled, feeling her heart race. "In the meantime, I'll raise the heat." In more ways than one, she thought, her lips curling into a grin as she walked over to the portable heater, turning it up to its max setting.

The loft was spacious, with high ceilings that made it harder to keep warm. The wind howled against the windows, shaking the panes as the snow hit them, sticking wet to the glass. Maggie stood by the window, staring out at the snow-covered street below.

"Come here and look," she called out.

Daniel walked over and stood beside her, peering out. "Yeah," he said, "I can't even see my car." He exhaled sharply. "I'm sure Rose will understand. It's getting worse out there."

He got out his phone and tried to call. All he got was a loud electronic buzzing. He said, "Storm must have taken out the tower. There's no signal." he looked at his phone and said, "Yep, only 911 calls now. Shit."

Maggie said with a smile, "You want more of that monk ale?"

Daniel laughed, shaking his head. "Yeah, maybe I should stay after all."

Maggie bent down to the mini-fridge and pulled out another bottle. When she stood up and walked back to him, bottle in hand, there was a new kind of warmth between them—a shared understanding, a quiet acknowledgment of what was happening.

"Maybe you should," she said softly, handing him the bottle.

Daniel took it, his fingers brushing against hers again, lingering this time. Their eyes met, and the storm outside seemed to fade away, leaving only the two of them, locked in the warm glow of the loft as the snow fell in thick, heavy sheets beyond the windows.

Chapter 20

Daniel

His shirt was plastered to his chest because of the heat in the loft and nerves of having decided to stay. He pulled at it, trying to get some air against his skin. "Do you have a towel?"

She smiled at him and said, "Yes, but I kind of like seeing you sweaty."

During the exertions of the past few hours, he'd loosened his black tie, and it gave him a disheveled, casual look. She went to a laundry basket laden with clothes and pulled out a white dish towel. She handed it to him. He opened his shirt a bit and put the towel up to his neck, wiping away some sweat.

"You'll have to wash this later. You can use my washer I have in the basement. I don't know when I used it last, but it works."

"I don't mind," she went to him, held the towel up to her nose and sniffed. "Mmm..." she whispered.

"It's a sweaty towel," he said, looking horrified.

"It's you," she grinned.

"I never understood that."

"Understood what?"

"Why women like a sweaty man."

"It's a long story," she said. She went back to the laundry basket and dropped the towel, but not before smelling it again.

"We're going to be trapped here for a few hours," he said. "Why don't you explain."

"No," she said. "I can't, it's a 'Girl Code' thing."

He sighed, "Fine. I'll take your word for it."

"Good," She went to the bathroom and brought out her purse. "I have something for you, an early Christmas present."

"And here I am without your present. I could run downstairs and get it, if you want."

"No," she said, handing him a small red gummy bear candy. "I can wait til Christmas. No opening presents before the day, that's my motto."

"So, what's this?" he took the candy.

"I got to thinking about the other night," she explained. "When I snuck in and we—"

"Yeah," He put a hand through his hair and his face flushed. "Like I said, I'm sorry. I don't know what happened."

"I do. You were too much in your own head. The gummy helps with that."

"And what does it do?" He looked at the red gummy bear again.

"It relaxes you," she said. "I take them sometimes when stress gets to be too much and I need to relax. It's got a few milligrams of THC. It'll be fine."

"What if I don't want to take it?" he asked.

"Do you want to make love to me Daniel?"

"I do," he told her. "Yes."

"And I want you too. But I don't want to force you into anything that will make you doubt yourself."

"I'm not doubting myself," he went to her, kissed her forehead. He sighed. "So, this will help take me out of my head?"

"Yes," she said. "But only if you want it. Only if you want me."

"I do want you," he said. He ate the gummy bear. The sugary taste blended together with something earthy and tart. He swallowed.

She smiled. "See, that was easy. Now just sit back and relax. Here, have a drink."

He sipped some of the ale, swallowed. His stomach tingled. He blinked.

Something was happening in his stomach. He felt an otherworldly feeling, a lightness he'd never experienced before. His heart beat a little faster as nerves started taking over his body. He shuddered. He breathed in deep, exhaled, and said, "Is this how it's supposed to feel?" His tone was dubious.

"Relax," she said. She went to him and put her arms around his back. Her face went to his chest, and he heard her sniff again.

"I don't think I can relax," he explained. "My heart's beating really fast now, Maggie..."

"You'll be okay," she said, sensing his hesitation. "Just sit down."

He stepped away from her and went to the small red diner style table she'd set up in the middle of the room. He sat down on one of the red leather chairs a bit heavier than he meant to. His head had become light, his mind wandering to too many topics to form anything he was thinking into one coherent thought.

"How are you feeling now?" she asked, coming to him. She started taking off his tie.

He breathed in slowly, easily. "Happy," he said.

His arms went instinctively to her waist, and he held her there. He didn't stop her from taking off his tie. His mind divided into two camps, one that wanted her with everything he had, and the other that held onto a painful memory five years old. He tried to push her away, but his arms weren't responding to what his brain was telling them. "Wait."

She didn't seem to hear him, as her body pressed tighter to him. She opened a button on his shirt, then another. He let her.

"Daniel," she whispered in his ear. "We've been flirting and going back and forth for the past few weeks. I've seen the way you look at me. I've looked at you the same way. Why don't you want me?"

"I do," he looked up at her face and it was redder than it was a few minutes ago. His brain felt fuzzy, incoherent, yet alive. A part of her was right. Why wouldn't he want to feel pleasure? Why shouldn't he want to feel the weight of her on top of him? Then his mind fixed on a thought. "But you're too young."

"Older men date younger women all the time," she unbuttoned two more buttons. He let her. Her hands went into his bare skin and she played with the chest hairs. The sensations of her hands on him warmed his body, and he went to hold her wrists.

"Don't."

"I'm going to tell you something," she said. "I met you when I was a teenager, I thought you were handsome. I wanted you then. I want you now," she pulled his shirt open, bent down and kissed his neck. He let her.

His hands, previously working under his mental power, became instinctual. He reached up and held her face in his palms. "I want you too," he said. He kissed her, his mouth finding her soft lips warm and wanting. He pulled back. She smiled.

"There you go," she said. She kissed him back, and then their tongues met. He held her by the back of the neck as the wispy feel of her hair brushed his knuckles.

She sighed. He moaned in her mouth. His body was out of control, and his brain felt far away. Yes, he wanted her at this moment. Then another thought invaded him. A hospital room, a hand in his. A long beeping sound. Closed eyelids of a woman he'd just lost. He pulled away. He dropped his hands from her face and moved to stand up.

"What?" she asked.

Tears started flowing from his eyes. "I can't, Maggie, I just—"

"Daniel," she said, her voice calm yet hard. This stopped him. "I swear to God, you are the most frustrating man I've ever met."

"Listen," he said. "I have to tell you something." He wanted to explain it wasn't her, it wasn't anything she was doing. He tried to form the words, but he couldn't with her looking at him, her eyes cold, exasperated.

"I'm going to do something," she said after a few moments of silence. "I need you to trust me."

"Okay, but—"

"No buts. Do you trust me?"

"Yes," he answered. "I do."

"Good," she wrapped the black tie around his eyes and tied it around the back of his head. "Relax." her voice was far away, even though she stood only a few inches from him. He could smell her rose and sweat musk and breathed. He couldn't see anything. He heard a dress fall to the floor, his senses seemed heightened, and he felt the cotton cloth of a shirt grazing over naked skin. That was put on the table in front of him. She pushed her breast into his face. "Lick me," she said.

"Mag-" She slapped him. It was a faraway pain, and he slouched away from her.

"Call me Cassandra," she said. Her voice had changed. No longer the young woman's voice he'd come to enjoy.

"What?" he was confused. "Mag—"

There was another slap, harder this time. "No!" she demanded. "Call me Cassandra."

"Okay," he agreed. "Cassandra, what are you doing?"

"Daniel, trust me." came her voice from behind him. He felt her move her face to his neck and gave slight wet kisses to his shoulder blade. "Remember when I used to do this to you, darling?" she purred in his ear.

He was lost now, confused, not knowing what was real or imagined. "Yes," he sighed. "Yes, darling."

"I've missed you so much, my dear," she said. His mind conjured a woman from memory, dark-haired, full lips smiling, kissing his neck now.

"Oh my god, I've missed you so much," a tear fell down his cheek. Fingers tousled his hair, and he felt the woman move around to his front.

"Remember when we used to do this, darling?" the woman's voice asked. He felt hands move down his naked torso, fingers undoing his belt. He let the woman do what she was doing. "Cass," he said. "Of course I do." His brain was a million miles away, his body was here, the sensations mixing to increase his desire for the woman who was taking off his belt, undoing the snap on his pants, pulling down the zipper.

His cock tightened against the white briefs he wore. He heard a slurping noise, as if a palm were being dragged over a moist tongue. Lips met his, and her voice said a long way away, "I've missed kissing you, my dear."

He reached up to the woman's hair, pulled her into a kiss, and kept his mouth on hers. A wet palm came down his shorts and rubbed against his length, then two fingers pinched the head, making him jump as a jolt of pleasure shot through him.

"I've missed kissing you too, dear," she said. Her hand went up and down on his shaft, wet, tight, stroking him.

"Darling," he panted.

"Let go, Daniel," said the woman's voice. "Let go, give yourself to me, one more time. One last time."

"Yes," was all he could say.

He took a deep breath in and exhaled, allowing his thoughts to drift away. He felt his body respond then, and only his body was in charge. Whatever she was doing, the continued kissing, stroking, talking, had the hypnotic effect of making him completely obedient to her. And he let himself become obedient.

The stroking continued and his cock grew harder in her touch. The wetness of her saliva on her palm formed a natural lubricant. He moved his hips up to her continued touch, as both hands gripped his cock firmly and went up and down in unison.

"Cassie," he breathed. His pleasure grew from the base of his balls and he could feel the tightness growing as he became harder.

Then lips kissed the head of his penis, and he shuddered. Then a mouth, wet and wanting, enveloped his cock, and the woman's mouth went down to the base of him. A hand grasped his testicles, squeezed, and her tongue glanced over the base of his head. He could feel pre-cum spill out from the tip as she pulled back. The suction of her mouth and cheeks pulled more of his essence out, and he was soon ejaculating in her mouth. He heard a satisfied pleasurable sound as the come erupted from him and he let out a hard groan. He had never come this fast. It had been too long since he'd had an orgasm. Far too long.

She came up to him, her naked body pressing into his face. Her tits met his tongue, and he lapped at the sensuous taste of her skin. She kissed him, and he tasted the salty, tangy essence on her tongue and lips.

Then he felt her sit down on him. The weight of her holding him in place, her weight comforting him. He wanted to cry, but was enveloped by the closeness of her skin against his. He felt the moist folds of her wanting pussy on top of his ebbing cock, and she gyrated atop him, pushing back and forth on top of him. He heard her breath, lusty, wanting, hungry.

He held her hips there and pushed her back and forth on him. Her wetness spilled onto him, dripping to his waist. He could smell the womanly musk of her. His mind kept him far away from thought, his body was responding again.

"Do you want me, Daniel?" her voice was far off but close simultaneously. What is she doing to me? He thought.

"Yes," he said. "I want to be inside you."

He felt her rise, then her slight tight fingers around his cock entered her, and she pushed down on top of him as his cock entered her all the way inside, so she rested fully on him. His cock jerked inside of her and the walls pulsed around him tighter by the second. She pushed forward, then up and then down, and he gripped her hips tighter. He was lost in her, in the sensations of her skin, her long slow kisses, her body trembling on him. Her breathy grunts and moans were music, and he added to that symphony with his own.

And he didn't care anymore. He wanted to be. He wanted all of her now. He was gone, in his body, fully embracing this carnal act.

Still penetrating her, he lifted to take her by the waist. She held his shoulders as he picked her up and moved her to the bed, not wanting to break the connection, he pulled the tie off and saw her naked in front of him. He looked down at his cock inside of her. The candle light of the room cast long shadows on his body along the wall and he grunted with pleasure, pushing into her again and again, taking her.

His body moved with a grace and heaviness that was undeniably primal. He couldn't stop himself now. He was there. She was beneath him. He lifted her thighs apart and pushed with all of his might deeper and deeper into her, taking this jewel in front of him, her blue blonde hair splayed out behind her. Her arms gripped the pillow behind her and she moaned and jerked her hips, meeting his, the slapping of skin blending with their lusty moans and grunts.

With his hands on her hips, he smashed into her, colliding with her in animal grunts. He became lost in her skin, the desire cascading through him. He pushed her up further on the bed and knelt in front of her. She grabbed his arms, pulled him closer, and their lips clashed. He couldn't get enough of her kiss. She wrapped her arms around his back. Her legs moved to his ass and her feet locked together. He couldn't stop fucking her now if he'd tried. He didn't want this feeling to stop. Neither did she. She propelled him closer to oblivion. And he still didn't want to stop. An animal lust grew in him. She was his. He was a caveman now, pulling her hair, biting her flesh. Taking her body. She was his cave woman, letting him claim her body and soul.

He stopped and pulled out of her. Her body belonged to him, and he pulled her up and turned her over on the bed. Her hips pushed against him, and he entered her, force and lust propelling his cock all the way inside. She grunted with release and he felt her insides grasp him, not letting go of his shaft. He held her down on the bed, his hand holding her hair, wanton and hard.

He heard her say his name, a far-off sound. His mind was gone. The sensations of want propelled him to lusty heights. He pulled her up by the hair and her body crashed against his. He held her by the throat, taking, fucking, pulling hair and kissed her as the last of his energy spilled out into her again. He never knew he'd had it in him to come twice in such a small amount of time, but he didn't care. He was going to claim her, his mate, his goddess, his possession. She was his. He was hers. This beautiful thing was now his possession.

She climaxed with a beautiful groan that made him spill deeper into her. He made noises he hadn't made in years, biting her throat, his heavy breath in her ear, his tight fist gripping her hair.

She collapsed in front of him and he finished watching the arch of her back push into the mattress. He went down and kissed the exquisite line in the middle of her back over and over. His heart beat with exertion and he tried to breathe, but couldn't. He collapsed on top of her. His cock was still hard inside of her. She looked over her shoulder at him. They kissed. Her breath returned to normal. A sheen of sweat glowed in the candle light, a beatific smile on her face.

"Wow," was all she could say.

"Yeah," His breath returned to normal. "Wow."

She turned to lie on her side and he followed, spooning behind her. He moved out of her and she groaned with disappointment.

"Sorry, I lost control there," he didn't know why he whispered, as if prying ears would hear them.

"Don't worry about that," she turned back to look at him. She wiped some sweat from his brow and licked her fingers. "Don't worry at all. I liked it."

"Still," he started to say, but she cut him off with a kiss.

"I liked it, Daniel," she looked him earnestly. "That's all you need to know."

"Okay," he said, and they kissed again. Then he smiled, and the smile turned into a chuckle. He didn't know what was happening. Joy filled his heart. He started laughing. It was a deep laugh, a releasing kind of hearty guffaw he'd not had in a long time, not since before his wife had died. She watched him like a lunatic, smiling at the apparent joy he was feeling for the first time in forever. Then tears came at the end.

"What was that?" She asked, wiping away the tears.

"Joy," he said finally, his shuddering breath easing as he allowed the last of his happiness to flow through him. "I'm happy."

"Good," she said. "I'm glad to hear it. It's about time, don't you think?"

"Yes. I think so. I forgot how good that felt."

"So, you liked it what I did?"

"Yes, I did. And now I want to do it again."

"Hold on there, tiger, let me catch my breath," she put her hand on his chest. "And you need to get your heart rate back down."

"Thank you."

"I have a question."

"What's that?" He was still far away in his mind, unable to reconcile what they'd just done.

"What's my name?"

Blindly he said, "Cass—"

She slapped him. "No." He looked at her like she'd just lost her mind. "I'm not her anymore. I'm Maggie."

"Okay, Maggie."

"You don't get to call me Cassandra anymore."

"I won't," He kissed her.

"Promise?"

"Cross my heart and hope to die."

"Well, we don't need to go to that extreme, but I get your point," she smirked.

He held out his pinky, and she did the same. They wrapped their fingers around each other and shook.

"Now that we have that settled, how about something to drink?"

"That would be great, Magpie,"

"Good, I'll go get it, Danny boy." She got out of bed and padded across the loft to the refrigerator. He watched her voluptuous body sway and move in all the right ways. She looked out the window after getting a bottle of water and said, "Well, looks like it's going to go all night."

"Speaking of going all night," he joked. "What time is it?"

"Twelve oh five," she said, looking down at her phone on the counter. "Merry Christmas."

He leaned against the pillows on the wall. She went to one of the boxes and found a red gnome hat with a white puffy brim and a fur ball at the top. She put it on with a flirtatious smile.

"Why don't you come over here and give me my present, Mrs. Claus?"

"Okay, Santa, baby," she giggled and skipped to the bed. She got in and sidled up to him. He put his arm around her back. They shared the water, and she set it on the wicker night stand next to the bed.

He looked at her, kissed her again, and said, "Best Christmas ever."

"Let's see what tomorrow brings," she moved against him.

"Yes," he said, caressing her breasts. "Let's." She moaned at his touch. "In the meantime, I'm not that tired." He hinted and pulled her close. He kissed her long and deep, and moved his hand to her ass.

"Oh, Santa," she sighed as she moved on top of him. "Do I need to put you on the naughty list?"

"Never."

Chapter 21

Daniel

The snow still fell outside the window when Daniel opened his eyes the next morning. As he awoke in her bed, memories of their passionate night together drifted into his mind, bringing a smile to his face. He looked over at her sleeping body—warm, exquisite, and soft, spooned into him. He bent his head to kiss her on the back, and she roused, moving her body closer to him.

He couldn't believe his luck. I could stay here all morning like this, he thought. Wrapped up in this woman's arms. A sliver of guilt swept through him, and he instantly regretted that it wasn't Cassie lying next to him.

So, this is what moving on feels like. He considered getting up, getting dressed, and going downstairs to see if he could leave and safely drive to Rose's house. A small part of him wanted to, but a larger part of him wanted to stay. He readjusted to lie on his back, staring up at the ceiling. The light from the mini blinds shaded the small bedroom and cast wan shadows across the ceiling. What am I doing? He asked himself. I shouldn't be doing this. He pulled the blankets up to his chest and put his hand over his heart. He felt the slow heartbeats and realized he was still alive. What did I think would happen, that a ghost of my wife would come down from heaven and smite me? A part of him was scared this might actually happen.

Bill would say, "You haven't done anything wrong." And he would agree. But the next time he saw the portrait of Cassandra sitting on the small shrine he'd made at his bookshop next to the cash register, he knew guilt would hit him like a lead pipe.

He felt her move, turn over, and lay a hand across his chest. "Hey," she said, her sleepy voice intruding on his thoughts. "Good morning."

He looked at her blue-blonde hair, moved it from her face, and bent to kiss her on the forehead. "Good morning, Magpie," he whispered. "Sleep okay?"

"Excellent," she said, kissing his chest and looking up at him. "You?"

"Best I've had in years. I guess I have you to thank for that."

"I'll take that as a compliment."

"So, do you know what day it is?"

She mocked an English accent and said, "Today? Why, it's Christmas Day."

He gave his best old man's voice and followed up with, "An intelligent boy, a bright boy."

She laughed. "I need coffee."

"So do I." He sat up and pushed himself against the pillows. Maggie sat up, revealing her naked torso and the pink-nippled breasts she had given him last night. Then she slid out of the bed, naked, and he watched as she moved to the kitchenette counter where the K-Cup machine sat.

"Sure you don't want to get dressed?" he asked, feeling a little embarrassed watching her nakedness move across the loft.

She turned and said, "Why would I do that?"

His face flushed, and he stayed silent. But he didn't stop looking at her.

"Thoughts?" she asked as the first cup of coffee started pouring into the white mug she'd set underneath.

"No." He lay back down on the bed and looked up at the ceiling. For some reason, he felt voyeuristic, scandalous even.

She reached for a mug in the cupboard. This is awkward, he thought. I should say something. But she broke the silence.

"Daniel," she said, still looking at the coffeemaker. "I like you. I like what we did last night. You're a good guy; no one disputes that." She turned to look at him. Her naked body took up his gaze—the curves of her breasts and hips, and the manicured V of her pubic mound. He admired her legs, the large thighs, and her fertile, essential womanhood.

"I like you, too," he said. His face felt hot all of a sudden, like he was looking at something that shamed him. "And I liked what we did last night, too."

"So, what's the problem?"

He didn't have an answer. He lay back down and stared at the ceiling.

"You were saying?" she prompted as the first cup of coffee finished brewing and she placed the next mug for another cup.

"Nothing," he said.

"Bullshit. Tell me what's on your mind."

"I don't know if you want to hear it."

"I do."

He paused. He couldn't explain what was on his mind, unsure of what actually was on his mind. But he started anyway. "I don't know what happens next. That's all."

She went to the refrigerator, pulled out a peppermint creamer, and poured it into the cups. "What happens next is we drink coffee and wake up. Then we talk about the snow. We talk about Christmas. We talk about memories. We talk about anything except what we did last night and how ashamed you might feel about it."

"I'm not ashamed," he said.

"Yes, you are. I can tell." She brought the cups back to bed. She handed him one and took a sip, breathing in the scent of it. He took a sip, too. They sat in silence for a few minutes, letting the magic of coffee do its work.

"Listen," he said. "It's been five years for me. The last person I did that with was my wife. It just feels wrong somehow."

"Why is that?"

"I don't know. It's like she's watching me, judging me. And I feel like I took advantage of you, is all."

"Did I fuck you?" she asked.

"Yes," he laughed. "Yes, you did."

"And you fucked me, too. Very well, I might add. So, it was consensual. You didn't take advantage of me. You made love to me, and I made love to you." She pointed to the ceiling. "And she was probably happy for you, so shut up."

"I'd like to think that."

"I know it." She took a long swig of coffee and sat against the pillows. She placed her cup on the wicker nightstand and leaned over to kiss him. He let her. Their tongues met. She tasted like peppermint and chocolate.

"Yummy," he said. "If you keep doing that, I'm going to want a repeat of last night."

"That's the spirit," she said, placing her cold fingers on his chest. He took her hands in his to warm them.

"You've made your point," he said.

"Good." She took another sip of coffee and stepped out of bed again. "I have to go to the bathroom, and I know you probably do too. Then maybe I'll break open that bag of bagels and look at the snow. I think we're going to be here for a while."

"And after that?" he asked as she walked toward the small bathroom door.

"Maybe an encore of last night." She looked over her shoulder and shook her hips as she closed the door.

He took a swig of peppermint coffee and sighed. In for a penny, he thought.

Later, after a breakfast of bagels and cream cheese, they opened the blinds to the small window that looked out over a snowy street. The blizzard still raged, making them feel like the only people on earth in a white veiled landscape. They made long and slow love. As she rose on top of him and he put his mouth on her breasts, she moaned above him. The last of the guilt of having her carnal embrace left his body, and he exploded with her, releasing it with a breathy groan. They slept again while the storm raged. They spooned in a sleepy embrace as the falling snow embraced the world around them.

When they woke up in the afternoon, the snow had stopped. Bright midday sun streamed through the window, waking them at the same time. His hand rested on her stomach, and he moved it down to her hip, feeling the softness of her skin. She murmured happily as she came out of a dreamless sleep.

"I could do this all day," she whispered.

"So could I." He kissed her back, and she arched to get closer to his lips. "I haven't had a day like this in a long time. I almost don't want it to end."

"Would it be wrong to say I don't want it to either?" he asked.

"Not at all."

He sat up, and she moved to embrace him, lying next to his naked body with her hand on his chest. He put his arm around her back and pulled her in close.

"You've got cute gray chest hair," she teased, tickling his hair and pulling it lightly.

"That feels good," he sighed.

"Something you like," she kissed his nipple. "I'll remember that."

A few silent minutes passed before she finally asked, "So, what's your favorite Christmas?"

"My favorite Christmas?" he looked at her, perplexed. "Where did that come from?"

"Curiosity, that's all. I mean, you must have one, right? Everyone does."

"I do, in fact," he chuckled, recalling a memory he hadn't thought about in years.

"So, spill it," she said.

"Okay," he said. "I don't know how much of a storyteller I'll be, but follow me, would you?"

"I'm all ears." She rested her head on his chest, still playing with his gray hairs as he talked.

"Well, it goes like this. We were here, in Newton's Crossing—I think I was ten. You know I've got two sisters, and the times leading up to Christmas were a bit tough. For the family, I mean. Dad had been laid off from the engineering firm and couldn't find a job to save his life. He wasn't going to work at McDonald's or fast food because that wouldn't pay the bills. He did everything he could—mowing lawns, helping neighbors for ten or twenty bucks, all kinds of odd jobs. He even took a job selling funeral plots for Golden Gardens, if you can believe that."

"They have cemetery plot salesmen?" she laughed in disbelief.

"Yeah, I didn't know that either. But what did I know? I was ten. All I cared about was Legos and playing cops and robbers with my friends."

"So, Christmas was rough. I get it. Go on."

"We were almost about to lose the house. Things looked grim. We didn't even have money for Christmas dinner—it was going to be sandwiches or leftovers that night. Every year up to that point, we'd had a Swedish cake log as a tradition, and Vernor's ginger ale. It was a big thing, waiting for Santa Claus."

He became lost in the memory now, recalling the disappointing two days before Christmas, when his parents broke the news.

"So, a few days before Christmas, Mom sat us down and said we wouldn't be celebrating. No tree, no lights on the porch, no presents. Santa was skipping our house that year. I still remember her breaking the news, tears in her eyes as she had to disappoint her kids.

"Of course, I was devastated. I had a long list of things I wanted, and at the top was a five-hundred-piece Lego set. I had such high hopes."

She said, "I want a Lego set right now."

"That would be fun, wouldn't it?"

"So, what happened? This is pretty bleak, Danny boy."

"We went to bed that night. I didn't want to get up. My sisters woke up the next morning—Christmas Day—and went out of the bedroom. I shared a room with my next-oldest sister, Regina. That's when I heard something unexpected: joy.

"Regina came back to the bedroom. Mind you, I just wanted to stay in bed all day and feel sorry for myself. But I wasn't allowed to, not with my sister jumping for joy on the bed. 'You have to see!' she was exclaiming.

"I told her I didn't want to get up, but she practically pulled me out of bed. 'You just have to see!' she kept saying. I followed her out of the room and down the hall to the living room."

"I can only guess," Maggie said.

"In the corner was a Christmas tree, lit up with all the trimmings—tinsel, lights, the works. But the most astounding thing was the presents. The entire room, about a ten-by-twelve-foot space, was filled with boxes and gifts. I swear, I couldn't see the carpet.

"My other sisters, Lara, and May, were already digging through the boxes, trying to find gifts with their names."

"So, your parents lied? How mean."

"No," he said. "They didn't. Turns out the people in the neighborhood found out about our situation and chipped in to give us Christmas that year. I still remember what I got. Someone gave me a Washington Knights sweater—why I'm a fan, by the way. I got a soundtrack album to The Sound of Music—I know, silly, but whatever, I liked Julie Andrews. Voice of an angel. I also got a Dick Tracy junior inspector kit with a light-up wristwatch, a bucket of green army men, and a few other things."

"What about the Lego set?"

"Ah, thanks for interrupting. I got the big set—the thousand-piece set—much to my father's dismay later on when he stepped on the pieces in the middle of the night."

"That's so sweet," she said. "I'm going to cry."

"They also brought a big turkey and all the fixings for dinner. It was a regular Scrooge and Cratchit moment. It renewed our faith in humanity. People looking out for each other—that's what Christmas means to me."

"So nice," she said. "I would never forget that Christmas."

"I haven't," he said. "That's why every year, I donate to Toys for Tots and other charities. Just to give back for that one act of kindness. Every year, I adopt a family and do for them what was done for us."

"You're a good guy, Daniel." She kissed him. He kissed her back.

"What's your favorite Christmas?" he asked.

"My dad was rich," she said. "Every year, I got whatever I wanted. We'd go to Aspen, or Europe, or some other far-flung place, and he'd shower us with gifts. But every year, a month later, I'd have forgotten all about it. The years blend together into unmemorable moments. For me, Christmas is just another day where a guy I barely know gives me gifts I barely appreciate."

"That's sad," he said. He got up and went to the door. "There's something I forgot. Hang on." He left, and she heard him running down to the store.

She stood, went to the fridge, took out food, and placed it on a tray. Just as she returned to the bed, he came back up the steps, breathless.

"Take it slow, old man," she teased with a laugh. "I'm in no rush."

"I just wanted you to have this last week, but Bill made me wait." He handed her a package wrapped in silver paper with a green bow. She pulled away the bow and unwrapped it, sitting on the bed.

"A cardboard box," she chuckled. "How nice."

"Just open it, smart ass," he said.

She opened the top of the box and gasped. "No," she put her hand to her mouth. "You didn't."

"I did," he said, smiling. "Do you like it?"

"Oh, Daniel, you didn't have to." She pulled out the present and looked at it in the light.

She stacked two green leather-bound books on her lap. The leather creaked as she opened the first cover, decorated with gold filigree. The title was Wuthering Heights. She looked inside and saw the frontispiece, the old typography, and underneath, it said, 'American Edition. Tenth edition.'

The other book was Jane Eyre, from the same publisher and edition.

"Oh my god," she said. "This must have cost a fortune."

"Not as much as you'd think. I pulled a few strings with a friend in Raleigh." He reached over and kissed her. "Merry Christmas."

She sighed. "I was wrong about Christmas memories."

"What do you mean?"

"This is my favorite one now," she said. They ate, and she sat with him in bed, opened her favorite book, and started reading aloud. "1801—I have just returned from a visit to my landlord—the solitary neighbor that I shall be troubled with... "

She read into the night, and as the sun set, she finished reading, snuggled close to him. Together, they made that Christmas Day one they would remember for years to come.

Chapter 22

Maggie

The last customers had filed out of the store a few minutes before lunchtime, and Maggie stood behind the cash register. She looked out at the busy street, across the way, watching Bill go in the doors of La Perk. Seeing no more customers in the store, she went to the door and turned the open sign to closed. She locked the door, and said, "Lunch time, finally."

Daniel had finished stocking in one of the aisles. The science fiction and fantasy section finally looked the way he wanted. They had a sale running on all the books, at twenty-five percent.

"Let's hope this works," he said as she approached. "This rent bill is way too high this month. Fucking Snyder's son. His father would never have done this right before Christmas."

"Is that what's been bothering you lately?" she asked, sidling up to him. She put a warm hand on his upper arm and squeezed. He made a pleasing sound in the back of his throat and turned to her.

"Customers all gone?" he asked.

"Last ones just left. I turned the sign and locked the door." She kissed him on the cheek. "Ready for lunch?"

"Yes," he said. "What did you bring today?"

"Microwave Chicken Parm," she said. "Not much, but it's all I could afford."

"I really do have to give you a raise."

"I don't need that," she said. "I mean, I kind of do, but with this rent thing, I don't want to make it harder on you to keep me."

"I would never let you go, now." He kissed her, wrapped his arms around her waist. "You mean too much to the store. To me."

"How sweet," she folded into his embrace. "But Daniel, you can let me go, I'll survive, you know."

"I know that, but I don't want you to just survive."

"Then what do you want?"

Daniel remained silent. He let her go and started for the middle of the store, where a large leather couch sat in a small reading area. Books had been piled on the brown leather sofa, a mix of classics, travel books, and Sue Grafton mysteries a customer was reading, then left behind instead of reshelving. "We'll have to put these back. I wish people would do that." he sighed. "Sometimes I hate customers."

"Changing the subject on me, huh?"

"What's that?"

"I asked you a question, Danny boy."

"And I didn't answer," he looked at her, then picked up some books and put them under his arm.

"Why not?"

"I don't have an answer, to be perfectly honest." He walked a few feet past her and she grabbed his arm.

"It's a perfectly valid question," she said. "And you do know the answer, you're just not telling me. What are you afraid of?"

"Who says I'm afraid?" His tone was defensive now, and he answered more harshly than he wanted to.

"Well?" she asked, not taking her hand off of his arm, looking pointedly in his eyes.

"Can we not talk about this now?"

"Nobody's around, I think it's a perfect time to talk about it. What do you want for me?"

"Maggie, I—"

"You like me, right? I mean obviously, you do. If Christmas was any indication. Can I assume you want me to stick around?"

"Yes," he sighed, "Yes, I do. But I don't want it to be a hardship for you. I don't know what you gave up to be here, I don't know why you came in to take this job. I had money to pay an employee, and now I don't."

"So don't pay me this week," she said. "Pay the rent. Keep the store open."

"But what about you? Jesus, chicken parm this week, what'll it be next week, fucking ramen?"

"If it takes that, yes."

"But it shouldn't fucking have to," he said. "An employer should be able to pay the people that work for him."

"So, I'm just an employee, now, is that it?" She chuffed and walked away. She turned back to him, her face red. "Is that what I am, just another employee? How many have you fucked then?" His effusiveness was getting under her skin.

"None!" he said, clearly off balance by her questions. "What do you mean by that question?"

"It's just," she stepped back from him. "I'm trying to give you an out. Trying to help you, giving you a chance to get your head above water with this shop. I like you a lot, Daniel. Enough to struggle for a few weeks to help you to keep the only place I like in this town open. You got it?"

She noticed his posture soften. "Yes," he said. "I get it. Sorry I got upset."

She went to him, gave him a long hug, and buried her face in his chest. "You're a great guy, Daniel. Caring, loving, honest." She reached up and grabbed his face. "But you're fucking frustrating sometimes."

"Takes one to know one," he laughed. He kissed her, opening his mouth and their tongues met.

"So," she looked around at the empty store and took the books from his hand. "Nobody here, we've got a few minutes..." Her voice trailed off with a wicked smile. Still looking him in the eyes, she dropped the books at his feet. "Oops, dropped them."

"You did that on purpose." His hands went around her waist and he pulled her closer. Still kissing her, he moved his hands down to caress her ample buttocks. She moaned in his mouth.

"Mayhaps I did," she reached behind her neck and undid the tie holding her wrap dress. "And mayhaps I didn't." The dress dropped to her waist, revealing her breasts.

"Guess I'll have to pick them up," he said, kneeling down on the floor. He kissed one nipple, then the other. She held the back of his head to her skin as his tongue played with both of them and his hands caressed her tits.

"Oh, you're smooth," she said.

"So are you," he put his face in her cleavage and licked. She moaned.

"I could get used to that," she moaned. He pulled down her dress, revealing her pink panties. He kissed down her stomach, then looked around at the open window, saw that no one from the street could see what they were doing, but decided to move to a more private place and lifted her up in his arms. She whispered, "Where are you taking me?"

"Trying to get away from prying eyes," he said. He went to the couch and laid her down, then pushed aside the Travel Coffee table books and relaxed on top of her in an instant. She opened her bare legs to him, wrapped one around his butt, and pulled him closer.

"Too many clothes," she said, and pulled off his button-down shirt. She loved looking at the gray and back mix of hairs on his chest, and she kissed his nipples. He gasped as her mouth found them, and he started pulling at his belt with one hand, the other resting atop her.

She reached down and said, "I'll help." Within seconds, she had taken off his belt and dropped it to the floor. She pulled his khakis down and stroked him. He was already hard, and her fingers found his girth.

He kissed her, then moved down on the cramped sofa to pull her panties down, seeing the promised V of flesh he'd enjoyed a few nights ago. She arched her back up to him as his mouth found her folds and opened them. "Yes," she sighed.

He found her nub with his tongue and slicked up and down on it. Fingers pushed inside, first one, then two, slick with her wetness. "Oh, my God," she cried, holding his dark-haired head to her pussy, as his tongue flicked and twirled on her clit. "Jesus, keep that up. Oh God!" The sensations filled her body with warmth, flooding desire through her. The things this man could do with his tongue defied anything any other man had done to her. His rhythm grew faster, and she bucked her hips to his mouth. The fingers in side went back and forth on her G spot and soon she was gasping his name, coming in his mouth, flooding the couch with wetness.

"I need you," she moaned. "God, I need you so bad."

"Goes both ways," he smiled, coming up to lie on top of her, his solid body pushing her into the couch. She held his cock and stroked it harder, and then he was inside of her, pushing deeper, thrusting, heaving, sighing on top of her. She wrapped her legs around his back and held him tight against her hot flesh. She purred as his groans and grunts filled her ears.

The rapid slapping of flesh against flesh was all the books could hear as their moans filled the reading space. He pulled back from her, opened her legs wide, and with a carnal lust kept ramming into her, she looked down at him penetrating her, the sensations of his cock hard and hot inside of her and she burst with a cry.

Her inner walls wrapped tight around him, and she gasped as he continued his cock's relentless assault.

"So tight," he said. "I'm so close."

"Give it to me," she moaned. "I can feel it, give it to me Daniel, give it to me!"

He could hold no longer, and fell on top of her with a liquid grunt that felt like everything he was poured into her. She wrapped her arms around his back, pulling him closer, as the last of his seed filled her, and they melted together, holding each other on the couch, spent, gasping for breath.

Neither spoke for several minutes. They simply held each other as his erection ebbed and softened inside of her. "A girl could get used to this," she said at last.

"So could a guy," he laughed and kissed her. Their breathing returned to normal, and they had to get up soon to open the store, but neither one wanted to.

"We have to re-open soon," she said.

"I know," he said. "Bill's going to be back from the coffee store and wonder why he can't get back in."

She laughed. "Doesn't he have a key?"

"Oh yeah," said Daniel. "But he hardly uses it. He has more keys on his keychain than I do."

"So, he could run the store the rest of the day?"

"Potentially, but he won't want to," Daniel shook his head. "He's just here for moral support, you know?"

"Yeah," she sat up. "I don't know why you let him hang around."

"He's a good friend, that's why," He explained as he came to sit next to her. He looked down at the couch and said, "We made a mess."

"We'll clean it up in a minute," she said, kissing him. She stood up and bent down to retrieve her dress. Daniel got dressed as well, and soon it was as if nothing had happened between them. He found her pink underwear on the floor.

"Don't you need these?" He raised an eyebrow and dangled them off of his index finger.

"You keep them," she smiled. "Something to remember me by, and if you want to take me sometime later, it's easier access," she bent down to pick up the travel books and put them on the couch. "If you catch my drift."

He slapped her on the ass and said, "Drift caught."

"Was hoping you'd say that."

She walked back to the register, set the books on the counter, and then went to turn the closed sign to open. Bill stood outside the door, key in hand, a perplexed expression on his face.

"Hey, Bill!" she said, a bit too cheerily.

"Uh huh," he said as he stalked past her. "Hope I don't have any messes to clean up later."

Daniel had heard this, and said, "No, Magpie here is going to do that in a few minutes, like the good girl she is, isn't that right?"

Maggie blushed, blinked, and smiled. "Whatever you say, boss."

Bill chuffed behind them, and as she turned to look at him, she saw a knowing smile on his face disappear. "Uh huh."

Chapter 23

Daniel

Workouts always gave him time to think. He ran on the treadmill, thinking about their relationship. For the past few days he'd been thinking about Maggie, what he was doing with her, if he was leading her on, if he was using her. Or if she was using him. He'd enjoyed their time together, obviously. Couldn't stop thinking about her, in fact.

He remembered the conversation he and Bill had had a week ago, before this relationship had gone any further. "You mount the woman, son." Bill had said in grandfatherly affectation.

When he ran on the treadmill, he always had his phone on a picturesque scene, following other joggers on mountain passes or pretty French villages. Today, he was cruising along Paris streets. The phone buzzed and showed Maggie's name. He let it ring a few times, wondering if he should pick it up. Finally, he hit the green answer button. "Hey," he said. "What's up?"

"Where are you? I'm at the store, and was thinking about lunch," Maggie answered.

"I'm just passing a coffee shop on the Champs Elysées."

"Paris today, the Alps tomorrow?" She asked knowingly. He'd told her at some point how he likes to work out, and she told him she'd thought it was cute. "Do you want lunch?"

"Sure. What are you thinking?" He slowed the machine to concentrate on her. He was almost done anyway, having spent twenty minutes on cardio at this point.

"Sausage," she laughed.

"You're lucky I'm in shape or I would have had a heart attack by now."

"Nah, keep taking your high blood pressure meds and you'll be okay." she said. "I promise I won't go too hard on you, old man."

"Old man, she says," God, he could get used to this woman. "Where do you want to eat?"

"Anywhere is fine."

"Ok. I'll cal you when I get done."

He ended the treadmill and went to a recumbent bike. He set up the phone to ride along the French Alps with a group of other bikers. The trail was long and steep, and at ten minutes in he was sweating, his brow furrowed, legs tight from the exertion of going up and down hills at the highest setting.

He believed in keeping his heart in shape at all costs, remembering an incident five years ago where he almost passed out because his blood pressure was too high. The doctor attributed his condition to stress, an unhealthy diet, and a sedentary lifestyle. Since then, he'd joined the gym, tried to eat right and stay healthy, and stayed away from sodas and fatty foods. He'd gone from over two hundred and fifty pounds to a healthy one ninety in that time. Yet every check up his doctor told him to keep up with the meds.

He ended his bike ride and went to the shower. The locker room was large, with deep red painted lockers along one wall with the same colored iron benches in front of them. He washed his face at the sink, looked at himself in the mirror and put wet hands in his hair. He didn't look too bad, he thought. A bit of gray at the temples, a few wisdom lines around his eyes, gray stubble. He'd thought of dyeing it at one time, but couldn't remember why he would do such a thing when he didn't have any reason to look any better than he did at present.

He always considered himself mid handsome, unforgettable in a plain sort of way. He never could understand why Cassandra had ever found him attractive. He made her laugh. That's what it was. And there she was, flickering into his mind again. Her red hair, the green eyes. The smile that said, "I love you," whenever she saw him. He shook his head, attempting to get her out of his mind, realizing he would never be able to.

He read a sign along one wall that told people not to leave belongings in the lockers overnight. He went to the shower and put his backpack on the black plastic chair. Pulling the red plastic curtain aside to protect his modesty, he took his gray sweat pants and tee shirt off. He started the water. The nozzle, an old discount hardware store shower head, trickled water. He sat on the black plastic chair and took off his socks. He put his hands under the water and felt it was hot enough to get under finally.

Taking the shampoo and soap out of his backpack, he put them on the shelf hanging in the white-tiled shower and started rinsing his body. He pulled a second red curtain closed and let the heat bask over him. Steam rose, and he breathed it in, relaxing him. He'd overdone it today, and his muscles ached. Another ibuprofen day, he thought. He washed his hair, then put soap on his body. The suds washed his body, and he relaxed a bit more. Daniel always liked being alone in the shower. It helped him think.

He heard the locker room door open, and he paid it no mind. He heard slight shuffling steps coming toward the shower. Seconds later, the outer curtain slid open.

"Occupied!" He cried out, wondering why they didn't hear the shower going and that someone was in there.

"I know," said a young chirpy woman's voice. Her. She pulled aside the curtain, revealing him naked, water running down his skin, suds in his hair. "Yummy."

She shucked off her pale blue yoga pants and Guns and Roses tee shirt, revealing her nakedness.

"What are you doing?" he hissed. "Are you nuts?"

"There's nobody in the gym. You picked a great time." She got into the shower with him.

"What are you doing? How did you get here?"

"Shush," Maggie kissed him, rubbing her wet naked body against him. He got hard. She stroked him harder and went down on her knees in front of him. She put the head of his cock in her mouth. He grabbed the back of her head.

"You're crazy," he moaned. "You know that?"

"Crazy for you, Dannyboy." She slobbered on him and got him harder than he'd been in a long time. He was fully aware of the scandalousness of this situation. He couldn't help but sigh, looking down at her marvelous naked form in front of him. He went along with it, hoping they could be quiet.

She stood up, and he lifted a leg to enter her while she held him. "Jesus, you're hard," she melted against him. "Oh my god. I should do this more often."

"Shush, someone will hear," he whispered, pushing deeper inside. She shuddered pleasurably against him. The water spilled over them in a wet cocoon.

"There's no one around. Keep going. Oh god, I'm gonna cum."

"Keep it down!"

Her moans echoed on the walls of the shower, and the outer walls of the locker room as the first orgasm hit her. "Jesus fuck!"

He heard something. Two men entered the locker room, talking. He pushed her up against the wall, set her on the shower handicap bar still inside of her, rigid and unmoving. She gyrated on him as he clamped a hand over her mouth to keep her from saying anything.

"How about that Longhorn's game yesterday?" one man said.

"Yeah, that quarterback they got is awesome. Did you see that eighty yard touchdown pass?" His companion asked. So far, they had heard nothing from the two lovebirds in the shower only a few feet away. Water splashing on tile was the only thing they heard.

"They're doing a lot better than last season."

"Right? How do you lose every fucking game?"

"Glad their coaches got fired."

"Yeah."

The first man asked toward the shower, "Hey are you gonna be in there all day?"

Daniel coughed, "Just getting done! Gimme a few minutes!" He looked at her eyes bulging and nostrils flaring as she tried to catch her breath. She closed her eyes, her body vibrated against him. "Finishing up now."

"Oh okay," the man said, clearly perturbed. "I guess I'll come back."

Daniel took a deep breath to calm himself. "There's another shower."

"Yeah, but I like to use that one."

"Got it," Daniel says, her eyes watered with imminent release. His cock throbbed inside her.

He coughed to slow himself down. His heart beat out of his chest and he swore the guy could hear.

"Okay, well," said the man. "I guess I'll take a shower after then."

"Yeah, I'll be right out, I promise." He felt he could barely hold his orgasm. If this guy didn't shut up, he'd be screaming in a few minutes, letting the entire gym know what he was doing.

"Nah it's ok. Have a good time."

"What?" Daniel thought. Why can't this guy just leave? He was about to burst.

"Take your time," the man said. "So who do you have on the Knights and Indians this week?" he asked his friend as they walked out.

"Oh, the Knights for sure," their voices receded and the locker room door closed behind them.

He took his hand off her mouth and she breathed in deep. She screamed in release as the orgasm burst through her like a charging bull.

She wrapped her arms around him, tugging him as her body bucked and shook against him.

"Jesus, I thought he would never leave," she said, when she had finally calmed down.

"I'm almost there," he said, and pushed deeper into her. Her legs wrap around his ass and he thrusts into her faster.

God, this woman is beautiful, he thought, watching the hot water dance along her brown nipples and course in runnels between her breasts and down her stomach as he slid in and out of her black, slick, wet pubic mound. He looked into her eyes and asked himself, "How did I get so lucky?"

He let himself loose as his moans and grunts echoed on the walls, their bodies slapping together as the shower water cascaded over them. He watched his cock ebb and flow inside of her, then pulled out, with her still on the handicap bar. He went down and licked her, his wet semen mixing with the water as it flowed out of her twitching pussy lips. He licked her clit to orgasm again, pushing his fingers inside of her. Her legs wrapped around his neck and she pulled his head forward, letting him taste her, lick her, feel his fingers inside of her. She came again, shocking him with the ferocity of her orgasm, spilling onto his face.

He stood, and they held each other, breathless, the water spilling down hot over their red flushed bodies. After a few moments, he caught his breath and asked, "Where do you want to go eat?"

"Anywhere but here," she put her head on his shoulder, licking water off of his skin.

"No, really."

She grabbed his cock again. "Anywhere I can get this."

"My place then?"

"Sure," she gave him a wink and a seductive smile.

He turned off the shower and, on shaky legs, got out and got dressed. She watched with contentment as he put on his clothes, opened the curtain, and looked out. He didn't see anyone. "Let's get out quick."

"You go first," she said, getting out of the shower to get dressed herself. He kissed her one last time and turned to the exit. He straightened, took a deep breath, and went into the hallway that led to the front exit. Another exit door loomed to the left, and he inexplicably neglected it, only to realize his mistake when it was already too late.

He went back into the main gym room with all the machines, shrugged his shoulders and saw the two men running on treadmills, engaged in conversation. "Done," he said. The man gave him a thumbs up and continued running. Daniel walked out, got in his car, and started it. "What the fuck was that?" he asked himself in the rear-view mirror.

Maggie came out a few minutes later. She had done the right thing and came out of the unseen exit, smiling as she saw him in his car. He smiled back.

He drove to the loft. She followed him there. For the next few days, they spent all the time they could together. It was the week after Christmas, and all through the loft, they stirred.

Chapter 24

Maggie

She had just finished the last sign on the bottom row of the fiction section when Daniel came back to see how she was doing. "Hey," he said, getting down on one knee behind her to see how the label looked. "How's it coming?"

Maggie had gotten a small label machine at the local office supply store, and it had been used to great effect in the Cookbook section, Paperback fantasy and sci-fi, and the self-help books. She looked back at him and said, "Going great. I'm done with this section. Now on to non-fiction. I didn't realize how big the store was when I agreed to this job."

"You convinced me to hire you, remember? I didn't offer."

"Stop," she scoffed. "You needed me. Admit it, Danny boy."

"More than you'd know," He came up behind her, and his arms stroked her back.

She turned, still on the floor, on hands and knees. "You need to stop."

"Or what?" he smiled, knee walking forward.

"It might lead to something," she smiled and came forward to kiss him. He returned the kiss, and their tongues met.

"So do I stop or go?"

"Is Bill still here?"

"Left ten minutes ago," he kept kissing her, then moved his mouth down to her neck. She purred. She planted a hot kiss on him, wrapped her arms around his back, and pulled him closer.

"Did you lock the door?"

"Would I be doing this if I didn't?" He pushed her multi-colored tie-dyed tee shirt up over her breasts, then went down with his mouth between her cleavage. She wore a green lace bra, and he pulled it aside, still kissing light pecks on her skin.

"I guess not," she moaned. She grabbed at his belt, pulling it apart, and then pulled the zipper of his khakis down rapidly. He went down on top of her, and she rolled him over to straddle him. She pulled up her green mini skirt and opened his fly.

"Aww," he said. "But I wanted to be on top." He reached up and unsnapped her bra with one quick motion and she let it drop, revealing pink buds. He lifted up and kissed them both. She held his head in her cleavage as she moved back and forth on top.

She felt his erection, and pushed him back down, then lifted on one leg, pulled her green lace matching panties aside, and impaled herself on his cock.

"Jesus, Maggie," he moaned. "So good, so so good..."

She was wet, and he slid in all the way, fast and hard. She felt him open her wider. She stopped, her body shuddering.

"Why do you make me want you so bad?" she kissed him, deep and longing.

"Feeling's mutual," He grabbed her hips and started moving her back and forth, rubbing her clit on his loins. Shudders and warm sensations went through her, and soon she couldn't help but kiss him hard, biting his lips in orgasm. Her breath came out in short gasps as her body tightened like a coil around his dick. "There's a good girl," he said.

Her face turned red, and she smiled wickedly, "That's right." Their bodies moved slower together, and soon she could feel his growing orgasm. "I don't want you to come yet."

"Neither do I," he nodded his head. "Let me take you from behind."

She lifted off of him, stayed kneeling on the gray carpeted floor, and he went behind her. He moved her skirt, pulled down her thong and took it off one leg, then he spread her cheeks wide, and pushed into her with a hard grunt.

"Oh, God," she moaned. He held her hips in both hands and she felt him jack hammer into her. All she could do was feel his length inside her, the muscles tightening around his shaft, and another orgasm spilling up her spine. "God, yes..." was all she repeated.

He pulled her hair, wrapping it in his palm, and pulled her up to feel her back on his chest. She opened her mouth to say something, but he stopped it with a sultry kiss as he nearly finished inside her.

"Keep going," she urged. That was all he needed to groan in her ear and collapse on her back as he filled her. She went down on bare elbows as he finished jerking inside, his shaft loosening her with come.

Their breathing slowed. That's when he heard a knock on the door.

"Shit," he said. "Who could that be?"

"Is that the key?" she asked, hearing something click in the door to the shop. "Dammit! Bill!"

"Fuck!" Daniel stood back up, putting his cock in his pants, and turned around to look at who had just opened the door. His hand fumbled for the belt, and it wouldn't snap fast enough.

"Dad?" a voice called from around the corner. "You here? The lights were on."

Maggie pulled quickly at her thong, getting it wrapped up as quickly as possible, and pulled down her shirt. She looked down, noting that her skirt was wet in the crotch area.

Daniel said, "Yeah, honey, hang on, I'll be right out."

But it was too late. Rose had come around the corner, red hair just as beautiful as her mother's, and saw them. Maggie was still on the ground, her bra next to her, shirt flung quickly over her breasts. Her father, putting his belt into the loop and looking flushed. "Hey," he said.

Rose stopped. She looked at Maggie. She looked back up to her father, noticed his guilty look and said, "What the actual fuck!?" She seemed rooted to the spot.

"Baby," Daniel said. "I can explain."

"I...," Rose's voice trailed away. Her face went ten shades of crimson. "What?"

Daniel grabbed at her, too forcefully he would later admit, and said, "Sweetie, I can explain."

"Explain what?" Rose raised her voice. "Explain how you're fucking my best friend from high school?"

"Rose," Maggie said, standing up. "It's all my fault. Don't blame your dad."

"Take your hands off of me," she pulled away from her father. "It's both your faults! Bullshit!" She turned on her friend. "Fuck off!"

"Hon," Daniel pleaded. "It's not what you think."

"I can't right now," Rose turned and started for the door. "I just can't with you two." She looked back at her father. "Don't call me! I don't want to talk to you!" She opened the door. The bell above the door rang. She left, slamming the door behind her. The bell rang even harder, punctuating Rose's anger.

Maggie and Daniel were silent for a minute. They looked at each other.

"Shit," Maggie said, breaking the silence. "She's pissed."

"She's a redhead," he said. "She goes from zero to a thousand in two point three seconds. I'll talk to her tomorrow. Give her time to cool off."

"Maybe you should go after her."

"Did you hear me say she's a redhead? I'd likely lose an eye," he looked down at his slackening cock. "Or something worse."

Maggie laughed, nerves overtaking her. He went to her and said, "It's okay, she'll be fine. It's just not what she expected to see when she came in."

"I guess not. Did you want me to talk to her?"

"Nah. I'll do it tomorrow. She'll be fine." He looked at the door, the bell cocked sideways by the force of the door slamming. "Or maybe not."

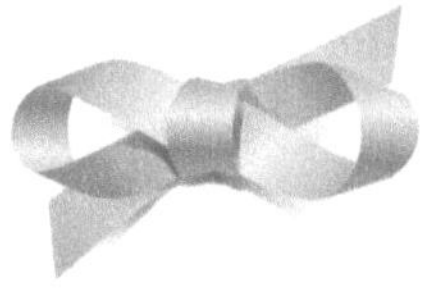

Chapter 25

Daniel

Rose's husband, Dave, answered the door after seeing Daniel's face on the video screen of their Ring doorbell. "Good afternoon," he said, ushering Daniel into the house. The two men had liked each other from the start, and Daniel had given his blessing to Dave when he came to ask for Rose's hand in marriage.

"How is she?" Daniel asked. Dave chuckled and shrugged.

"She's fine, I guess," he said. "She told me what happened."

"What do you think?"

"Dad, it's none of my business. Love is love, I figure."

"Where is she?"

"Out back." The two men walked through the kitchen of their White Pines home, with suburban white countertops and an island in the center. Daniel saw his daughter, her red hair blowing in the morning wind, sitting in the sunroom overlooking the large backyard. "Want some coffee?" Dave offered.

"No," Daniel said. "Best get on with it, I guess."

"I'm supposed to be mad at you too, you know," Dave said.

"Figured as much. Are you though?"

"Nah," Dave put his hand on Daniel's shoulder. "Got better things to do than worry about who's banging who. Didn't stop me from hearing about it for the last day and a half."

"Sorry about that."

Dave shrugged. "I'm a firefighter. I see and hear worse. I just listened to her vent, and she calmed down after a bit. But you might want to take a snack out to her." He picked up a peach from a bowl of mixed fruits in the center of the island and handed it to Daniel.

"Maybe it'll help, maybe not."

"Couldn't hurt."

Daniel walked to the large French doors that led to the sunroom. Through the windows he could see the remnants of the blizzard mixed with patches of green grass. It looked so serene; he almost believed his daughter had forgiven him.

"Hey," he said, seeing his daughter drinking her morning coffee from a cup that read, 'There's not enough blood in my coffee system'. She wore blue sweatpants and a long white T-shirt. He put his hand on her shoulder, and she rested her own hand on his.

"Hey," she replied. Her face was flushed from crying. "Did you want some coffee?"

"Dave asked me the same thing," he said, sitting down in a stuffed chair next to hers. "I brought you an apple." He handed her the juicy red fruit. She took it and bit into it.

"Thanks."

"You're welcome," he said, his tone cautious. "How are you doing?"

"Fine."

One-word answers. I see how this is going to go. "Rose," he began.

"How long?" she interrupted. "Before you start trying to explain this away, just tell me how long."

"Does it matter?"

"Yes, Dad, it fucking matters. I specifically asked you at Thanksgiving. Do you remember what you said?"

"I said no," he admitted, leaning forward. The overstuffed chair made it hard to have a proper conversation. Rose placed her coffee cup on the coffee table and turned angrily to him.

"You said no," she demanded. "Were you lying then?"

"No, I wasn't. What is this, Judge Judy all of a sudden?"

"Yes, it is. So, tell me how long."

"Since a little before Christmas," he said. "A few weeks before that, we..." He struggled to find the words. "Thanksgiving was our first kiss. But we were both tipsy, so we decided maybe it wasn't for the best."

"Obviously."

"But a few days later, we did something else, and it was fun—"

She raised a hand to stop him. "I don't need to know. Just stop."

"You asked!" He raised his voice.

"I just wanted to know how long you've been fucking my best friend!" She stood up, throwing the apple onto the table, and turned on him. "Was it back then? When you were with Mom?"

"Back then?" he stood, his anger rising. "When she was eighteen? What do you take me for?"

"You know, she told me you were cute. Even flirted with you once or twice. Right in front of me."

"So what? By that logic, you think I was sleeping with your eighteen-year-old classmate under your mom's nose? The woman I loved more than anything?"

"Yes, I kind of do!"

Her words stopped him cold. He clenched his fist, fighting back the urge to lash out. "I don't think we need to talk anymore, young lady," he said, using the term he always did when upset with her. "You're out of line."

She turned and leaned on the railing. "I'm sorry," she said after a moment, her voice softer. "Dad, I'm just... confused."

"What are you confused about?" He stepped closer, his anger fading as he placed his hands on her upper arms.

"Her. What you see in her. I just thought you wouldn't do anything with another woman after Mom. That's all."

"I didn't plan this, you know. It just... happened."

"Nothing 'just happens,' Dad."

"This did," he replied, staring out at the yard. "I told her on several occasions that it couldn't happen, that it would be too much for everyone involved."

"So why did you go ahead with it?"

His mind flashed back to that Christmas Eve. The oppressive loneliness. The lack of physical touch. "I missed your mother."

"And this is who you replace her with? My best friend? A woman eighteen years younger than you? I thought you were better than that."

"Well, apparently, I'm not."

"At least you admit it."

"Admit what?"

"That you're just like other men. You couldn't find someone your own age?"

"I wasn't looking."

"Then what made you do it? Why her?"

"She touched me," he said, remembering the way Maggie's hand had felt on his shoulder, his neck, the kisses on his cheek. "Look, I could sit here all day and try to justify everything, but if you want me to end it, I will."

"Do you, though?"

"Do I what?"

"Want to end it." Her eyes demanded the truth.

"No," he said, without hesitation.

She sagged against the railing. "Fuck."

"I know it's unconventional. Maybe even wrong. But we're two consenting adults, and we've talked about it. It's just a fling."

"She was my best friend!" Rose's face flushed with anger again. "She's a kid!"

"She's almost forty. Do I need to remind you of that?"

"She's two years older than me! You think I want a stepmom that's practically my age?"

"I'm not making her your stepmom. Jesus, you're reaching, hon."

"So, you're using her!"

"If anyone's using anyone, it's her using me. You think I asked for this?"

"You could've said no. Agreeing to it is just like asking!"

"Then we're using each other! Besides, it's just until the end of the year. She's already said she's going back to L.A. in January."

"So, she comes to town, you get your jollies, and then she leaves? And you go on with your life?"

"Yes."

"You're disgusting!" She stormed away. "I thought you were better than this."

"I am," he said, following her. "And don't turn your back on me, young lady. I'm still your father."

"'Father,'" she mocked, her back still to him. "She's young enough to be your daughter."

"You think I didn't consider that? The first time we kissed, I told her it couldn't happen."

"So, what changed?"

He remembered the excitement when Maggie had crawled into his bedroom window, the taste of her kisses, the softness of her naked skin. "Because I wanted her. Is that what you want to hear?" He shouted. "She wanted me, and I was lonely. She was the first woman who looked at me with desire since your mother died. So, I went for it. For five years, I closed off my heart, and she made me open it again. And I gave it to her."

"But did you think about me? How I'd feel?"

"I did. That was one of my hesitations."

"So, what changed? I just want to know why."

"She made me feel young again. Like when I first met your mom. I just wanted to feel happy again. After so long of being alone, with no one to hold. No one to love. No one to fuck for Christ's sake!"

"Eww." She turned to face him. "Gross."

"Sorry," he said, holding her arms gently. "We're upset. We're going to say things like that. I don't know what to do anymore."

She gave a soft chuckle, the tension easing. "I get it." He could feel her anger melting. "It's been tough for all of us. I'm sure you, most of all. It was just a shock seeing what I saw. I can't get it out of my mind."

"Sweetie, Maggie and I care about each other very much. She's a kind woman, and she's helped me in ways I can't even explain. This isn't one of those midlife crises you hear about. Our affection for each other is real."

Rose walked over to her father and hugged him around the waist, resting her head on his chest. He placed a hand gently on her head.

"So, she makes you happy?" she asked.

"In more ways than one," he replied.

"I'm sorry I got mad. I just needed to know. I had to hear it from you, I guess. It's just... hard to see," she admitted.

"I know, baby," he said, stroking her back. "I know."

"So, I guess you're looking for my approval then?"

"I don't need it," he said, "but I'd like it."

"If she makes you happy, who am I to tell you what to do with your life? But after she's gone, could you maybe date someone your own age, please?" she teased.

"I promise."

"Okay," she said, looking up at him. "Just have fun. Let her make you feel alive. Shit, you're my dad. I can't stay mad at you. And she is an adult, after all."

"Exactly," he agreed. "Two consenting adults having fun. And I'll never stop loving you either."

"I know," she said. She held him for a few more moments, feeling the tension between them fade away. Finally, she asked, "Want to stay for lunch? I made some of Mom's pickle and bologna salad."

"Yes, baby," he said, kissing her on the forehead. "I'd love to."

Chapter 26

Maggie

She held Daniel's hand as they watched the men finish setting up for the annual New Year's Eve pig drop. The PGSKNZ Pork Factory, a local fixture in Newton's Crossing, had been the heart of the town for years. Every year, they hosted this quirky event: at the stroke of midnight, a large, foam pig was dropped from a crane while the townspeople counted down. The event was more than just a spectacle—it was a celebration of the community. The owner of the factory, along with his wife, gave a speech thanking the town for its support over the years. The couple was well-loved in the community—he had served on the city council, and she ran charity events for the local Baptist church.

There were bags of free pork skins, a barbecue contest, and even toys for the kids. People gathered from all over, their breath visible in the cool night air as they waited for the countdown to begin.

Maggie glanced up at Daniel, who looked contemplative. "So, this is it, huh? Tomorrow, you leave?" he asked quietly, his voice almost drowned out by the noise of the crowd.

"I don't know if I really want to," she admitted, her grip tightening on his hand.

"Why not?"

She turned to him, her eyes soft. "Because, Daniel, if you haven't noticed, I kind of like you."

He smiled. "I kind of like you too."

"So, what do we do now?"

"I don't know."

"Can we figure that out tomorrow?" she suggested, looking toward the sky.

"Why not now?" he pressed.

"Because the fireworks are about to start, and I don't want to ruin the moment."

"We should've talked about it earlier," he said, the weight of the unspoken future hanging between them.

"That would've really ruined the moment," Maggie teased, but her smile faltered. "We knew this was temporary from the start."

Daniel looked away, his eyes scanning the crowd. "Something tells me you don't want it to be the end," she said.

"Would it be bad if I didn't?"

"No," she sighed. They stood in silence for a moment, the weight of it all pressing down on them. Maggie finally turned to him and said softly, "Can I tell you something that's been on my mind? And can you promise not to run away?"

Daniel gave her a small smile. "I promise."

She searched his eyes, making sure he meant it. "I think I've loved you since I was eighteen. The first time I saw you in your house, with Rose and Cassandra."

He didn't respond at first, his face unreadable.

"Well?" she asked, her heart pounding.

"Well, what?" Daniel said, a faint smile tugging at the corner of his mouth. "I'm sure it was just a schoolgirl crush. Why would you want to fall in love with me? And we're already in trouble with Rose as it is."

"Are you trying to push me away?" she asked, her voice tinged with frustration.

"No," he said softly. "I just... I want to know what a young woman like you sees in an old guy like me."

The crowd suddenly roared, the countdown beginning.

"Ten!" the voices outside shouted.

Maggie turned to face him fully, her eyes locking onto his. "You're kind. You're witty. You're smart. You're great in the sack." She grinned. "And you're tender. What's not to love?"

"Nine!"

Daniel blinked, taking in her words.

"The first day I saw you," Maggie continued, her voice firm, "you were devoted to your wife and daughter. You were so damn cute."

"Eight!"

"I don't know where this is going. I can't promise we won't grow apart."

"Seven!"

"I don't even know what I'm doing here. When I came to town, I promised myself I'd stay single. Live like a normal person. Just... wait for something to happen."

"Six!"

"But then you did," she said, her voice catching slightly. "You happened."

"Five!"

"And I don't want us to be apart."

"Four!"

Maggie leaned in and kissed him, soft and full of meaning. "Ever," she whispered.

"Three!"

Daniel wrapped his arms around her, pulling her close. "I don't want to be apart from you either," he murmured against her lips.

"Two!"

"Ever," he added, his voice thick as their eyes met.

"One!"

"I love you, Magpie," Daniel whispered, his voice barely audible over the roar of the crowd.

"I love you too, Danny boy."

As the foam pig dropped from the crane and the fireworks exploded overhead, they kissed again, this time with all the passion they had been holding back. The colors of the fireworks—yellow, red, blue, and white—reflected in the windows of the loft, casting a vibrant glow across their entwined bodies.

In that moment, the outside world disappeared. The courthouse was gone. The cheering voices were gone. All they saw and heard were the fireworks, as he pressed her against the window, and they made fireworks of their own.

The next day, they spent every moment together—lounging, watching TV, making love, and talking about their future. Maggie told him that she had to leave for Los Angeles. She had business to attend to.

"What if I go with you?" Daniel asked, not wanting to let her go.

"No," she said, shaking her head gently. "I have to do this myself. I've got unfinished business in the city. There's paperwork to sign, things I need to sort out with my old boss. It's a long story, but I'll be back in a few days."

"I won't worry, then."

Maggie smiled, though she could see the concern in his eyes. "Good."

But for the next few days, Daniel worried.

Chapter 27

Daniel

It was January third, and Daniel was on edge. He'd only heard from Maggie a few times over the past few days. Her texts were a mixture of, I'm still doing stuff, I'm busy, or I can't talk now, always ending with xoxo. They hadn't actually spoken since she got on the plane to Los Angeles, and every moment without her felt like torture. Seconds turned into minutes, minutes into hours.

I guess this is what happens when you love someone and they're away from you, he thought. He had never really experienced this with Cassandra, because they were always together. They took trips together, went to family gatherings together—there were no "girls' trips" for her or "boys' trips" for him. They were inseparable, best friends. Since the day they met, he never wanted to be out of her sight for more than a day.

And now, here he was, doing the same thing with Maggie.

Every time the bell above the door rang, his heart leaped, hoping it was her. Bill had noticed, and it was driving him nuts.

The bell rang again. Daniel looked up.

Bill sighed dramatically. "She's going to come back, you idiot. Would you stop that?"

But it was another customer, a tall man in a gray suit. The man's predatory eyes scanned the bookstore, taking in the changes Maggie had made: Christmas decorations still hung in the window, and twinkling lights crisscrossed along the tops of the shelves. She had turned the place into a winter wonderland, and every time Daniel saw the lights, he missed her a little more.

"Can I help you?" Daniel asked, his voice sharper than intended.

The man smoothed back his greasy black hair. Daniel's stomach sank when he realized who it was.

"Oh, you," Daniel muttered.

It was Ellis Marleigh. Ellis raised his hands in mock surrender, flashing a greasy smile. "Whoa, there. I know I'm not the most popular guy around, but hear me out, okay?"

"I have your rent money," Daniel said, reaching for an envelope on the desk, filled with cash. "I'll want a receipt."

"Wait a minute," Ellis said, waving his hands. "I'm not here for that."

Daniel exchanged a confused glance with Bill. "I'm sorry, what?"

Ellis leaned against the counter, still grinning. "No need for the rent. I don't own the place anymore."

"You... don't own it?" Daniel asked, baffled.

Ellis shook his head. "Nope. I've had this place on the market for a few months now, and someone finally bought it. So, you'll have to deal with the new owners when they get here today."

"Who's the new owner?" Daniel asked.

"No idea," Ellis said with a shrug. "All I know is my dad's realtor called with an offer on this place and some other properties we own. I took the deal. Real estate was never my thing, anyway. I'm more of a business guy. Now I've got the money to invest, maybe buy that beach house in the Keys I've always wanted."

"Good for you," Daniel muttered. "So, when will the new owner contact me?"

"No clue," Ellis said with a smirk. "But hey, keep your money. You'll probably need it."

"Thanks, I guess," Daniel replied, not hiding his irritation.

Ellis shot finger guns at him. "Catch you later, buckaroo. Good luck with the book biz! I'll think of you when I'm sipping Mai Tais on my private beach. Nah," he reconsidered with a laugh, "probably not. See ya."

He left, the bell jingling as the door closed behind him.

"Well, shit," Bill said, shaking his head. "New owner. Rent's probably going to go up."

"Good thing we did okay for Christmas," Daniel muttered. "But you know what the place looks like in January and February."

"Yeah, a fucking ghost town," Bill agreed.

He got up and walked to the back, grabbing a bottle of water from the fridge. As he wiped the condensation from the side and twisted the cap, the unmistakable roar of a muscle car engine echoed from outside. Daniel's brows furrowed. What the hell?

He walked to the front, just in time to see a cherry-red Mustang convertible with white leather interior screech to a halt in front of the store.

Of all the days to get bad news, now someone had to show up in his dream car to rub salt in the wound. Great, he thought. First, he finds out his rent situation is up in the air, and now this.

The driver stepped out—a woman in her late thirties, wearing a black hoodie and sunglasses. She had a briefcase in hand. Must be the new owner, Daniel thought bitterly. She looked young, attractive, probably some stuck-up corporate type. But something about her lips seemed familiar.

Then she pulled back her hoodie, revealing blonde hair with blue highlights. She took off her sunglasses.

It was Maggie.

Daniel's heart skipped a beat as she smiled and walked inside. Without a word, they hugged, and the hug quickly turned into a long kiss.

"Get a room, you two," Bill called from behind the counter. Maggie flipped him off with a grin.

"You're back!" Daniel exclaimed, breathless.

"Yes, I'm back. It's been a long few days. I'm exhausted, and jet lag is a bitch."

"Did you get all your business done?" Daniel asked.

"Yep." She pointed out the window toward the Mustang. "Merry Christmas."

"What do you mean?" Daniel asked, confused.

Maggie rolled her eyes playfully. "The car, Danny boy. Merry Christmas. It's got about a hundred thousand miles on it, but it's pristine. I bought it off some kid in Raleigh. Got a great deal."

His jaw dropped. "How did you buy a car? I don't pay you that much."

"It's a long story," she said, laughing. "I'll tell you in a minute. But first, I've got something else."

She pulled out a familiar-looking book—A Christmas Carol, the first edition Daniel had sold to a dealer from Raleigh.

"Merry Christmas number two," she said, handing it to him.

Daniel stared at the book in disbelief. "Maggie, what... what is going on? How did you get this back?"

"It's all part of the long story," she said, gently placing her hand on his arm. "Just calm down."

"I can't calm down! This is too much. I don't understand."

She smiled, pulling a leather satchel onto the counter and taking out a sheaf of paperwork with a blue cover. She handed it to him.

"What's this?" he asked, flipping through the pages.

He read the letterhead: Brooks and Associates Realty. As he skimmed the document, his eyes widened. "Margaret Thorne, owner of real property at..." His voice trailed off as he looked up at her, stunned.

Maggie beamed.

"You're the new owner?" he asked, incredulous.

"Yes," she said, smiling proudly.

"Of this building?"

"Yes," she said again, nodding.

Daniel looked over at Bill, who simply shrugged. "I'm as clueless as you are, man."

Daniel turned back to Maggie. "I don't get it."

"Okay, don't freak out," she said, pulling out a fountain pen. "Take a look at the signature line."

He glanced down. The owner's line was blank.

"I'm selling you this building," she explained. "This is the deed. All you need to do is sign on the dotted line, and it's yours. Merry Christmas."

"I can't," Daniel stammered. "This is ridiculous. You bought the building?"

"Yes," she repeated calmly. "But now I'm selling it to you."

She handed him the pen. He hesitated. "How much do I owe you?"

Maggie leaned in, her eyes twinkling with mischief. "Just a kiss. And maybe the rest of your life."

Daniel pulled her into a kiss, long and full of passion. When they finally pulled apart, he whispered, "I think I can do that."

He signed the papers, his heart pounding as he looked around the shop that, after all these years, was finally his. Maggie hugged him, and Bill made a face.

"You two are atrocious," Bill said with a grin, grabbing his scarf and hat. "I gotta go."

"You're not staying for the celebration?" Daniel asked.

"Nah," Bill said, shaking his head. "Something tells me, by the way you two are looking at each other, I don't want to be around for this one. Besides, I've spent enough time playing babysitter over the years." He nodded at Maggie. "It's your turn to babysit him now, sweetheart."

Maggie laughed. "Don't worry, I'm up to the task."

Daniel smiled. "I'm sure you are." They kissed again as Bill waved them off, pulling his scarf tighter against the cold.

"Congrats, my guy," Bill said, clapping Daniel on the back before heading out the door.

The bell jingled as the door shut behind him, leaving Daniel and Maggie alone in the quiet bookstore, surrounded by twinkling lights and the scent of old books.

"How?" Daniel asked, his brow furrowed. "I don't understand."

Maggie smiled and placed her hand on his arm. "Okay, you might want to sit down for this. It's going to take a minute, and trust me, you'll want to be seated."

He sat down on the couch, and Maggie followed, curling up close beside him. She hugged him tightly, resting her head on his shoulder. "I've missed you," she said softly.

"I've missed you too," he replied, squeezing her hand. "But what's going on? What gives?"

Maggie took a deep breath and leaned back. "Okay, so, when I was eighteen, my mom gave me some money from a trust fund. I wanted to be smart with it, so I invested it. But, being even smarter, I put a stipulation on the investments that I couldn't touch them for twenty years."

Daniel nodded, listening intently.

"Well, that twenty years ended a couple of days ago."

His eyes widened. "So... what did you invest in?"

Maggie's lips curled into a mischievous smile. "Only a little search engine and a social media platform that ended up doing really well."

"And those are?"

"Google and Facebook," she said, grinning. "I didn't expect them to blow up like they did. Who knew, huh?" She laughed. "With the initial investments and a few more over the years, it grew... well, to around ten million dollars."

Daniel's jaw dropped. He sat there, frozen. She gently pushed his chin up to close his mouth.

"So, when do we get married?" he joked, finally finding his voice.

"See, Danny boy," she teased, laughing. "That's why I didn't want to tell you. I knew you'd only want me for my money."

He shook his head, pulling her closer. "I want you for you," he said. "Always."

She melted into him, snuggling into his arms. "I feel the same way."

They sat in comfortable silence for a few moments, the weight of their future settling over them, warm and safe. Daniel had an idea and stood. He pulled her up with him.

"I think we're closed today," he said, his tone playful. He walked to the door.

"I like that idea," Maggie replied, following him.

Daniel looked out the door, flipped the sign to closed, and locked it. As he turned around, Maggie was right there, and he pulled her into a tight embrace.

"Merry Christmas, Magpie," he whispered against her hair.

"Right back at you, Danny boy," she replied softly.

Across the street at La Perk, Bill sat at his usual table, nursing his coffee as he gazed out the window at the bookstore. He watched as Daniel flipped the sign and pulled Maggie into his arms. Bill smiled to himself.

"Good for you," he murmured, sipping his coffee.

A familiar voice interrupted his thoughts. "Did you want another scone, Bill?"

Bill looked up to see Charlotte standing in front of him. She had short, curly black hair, a few soft wrinkles around her eyes, and a smile that could light up the room. He had admired her for the longest time, but now... now felt like the right moment.

Bill reached into his coat pocket and pulled out a single rose, holding it up to her with a hopeful grin. "You know what I want,

Charlotte? You and me, tonight, at Angelo's. Seven o'clock. What do you say?"

Charlotte's smile widened, and she glanced over at the bouquet of roses behind the counter—the ones she had been receiving week after week, not knowing who had sent them. Her eyes softened as she looked back at Bill.

"You?" she asked, her voice barely above a whisper.

Bill nodded. "Yes. It's Me."

"Yes," she said with a beaming smile, her voice filled with warmth. "Yes, I will."

Epilogue

The bookstore was alive with energy, brighter and more vibrant than it had ever been. The once dusty shelves were now sleek and polished, lined with colorful new titles. Soft, golden lights hung from the ceiling, casting a warm glow over the cozy reading nooks nestled into the corners. A few patrons sat quietly in the back, leafing through books, while the front of the store buzzed with the excitement of Daveon's first book signing.

Daveon signed another copy of his book, Companions of the Blade. The cover showcased four heroes facing off against a swirling, shadowy demon. He handed the book to the eager customer with a smile. "Thanks for coming," he said, "I hope you like it."

Daniel said, "It's really good, I got to be a beta reader. Had me on the edge of my seat the whole time."

Daveon said, "Thanks Dan. It's no Lord of the Rings, but it'll do, I guess."

"Don't' sell yourself short, buddy," Daniel gave him a pat on the shoulder. "You're a good writer. Keep it up."

The bell above the door chimed and in walked Bill, arm in arm with Charlotte. Bill wore his usual easygoing grin, but there was something lighter about him today—something that had changed in the months since he'd finally asked Charlotte out.

"Bill!" Daniel waved from across the store. "Good to see you two!"

Bill waved back, leading Charlotte toward the counter. "What? You think I was gonna miss this?" he said with a chuckle. "Not every day you get to see a local author sign his first book."

Daniel said, "It's good to see you two. How long did I tell you to ask her out?" He asked Bill.

Charlotte smiled warmly, squeezing Bill's arm. "You should have seen it. He was so cute," she said playfully, looking at Daniel. "Besides, if I had to throw another rose away, I was going to scream."

Everyone laughed, and Bill rolled his eyes, though the smile on his face never wavered. "Hey, it worked, didn't it?"

"Yes," Charlotte kissed him on the cheek. "It did."

As they moved to the side, Daniel caught sight of Maggie behind the counter, checking out a young woman who was excitedly clutching her newly purchased book.

"I love fantasy novels," the customer said as Maggie scanned the book. "I can't wait to read it."

"You're in for a treat. He's got two more coming out this year," she said, glancing over at Daveon and Sherise, "if he doesn't let the fame go to his head."

The customer laughed. "I'll be sure to keep an eye out."

Just then, a soft cry came from the back of the store—a tiny voice breaking through the bustle. Maggie glanced over at the baby carrier behind the counter. "Duty calls," she said with a smile, as she handed the customer her book.

Daniel stepped forward, gently lifting their daughter from the carrier. "It's okay, sweet girl. Daddy's got you."

The customer's face lit up as she watched Daniel cradle the baby. "Oh, how sweet! How old is she?"

"Three months," Daniel replied, pride swelling in his chest as he looked down at his daughter.

"She's adorable," the young woman said, her eyes softening. "What's her name?"

Without hesitation, Daniel and Maggie both answered in unison. "Cassandra."

. . ⁂ . .

The End
Merry Christmas Everyone.

Author's Note

I HAVE ALWAYS LOVED Christmas, no matter the religious or secular point you put on it, when people are good to each other, and love and generosity reign supreme. One of the stories in this book is true. In 1976, our family had fallen on rough times, the neighbors really did band together and give us the Christmas of our dreams. And yes, I got everything Daniel says he got. Except it was a Washington Redskins jersey, but since I can't say those names in a fictional sense, I had to change the name of the football team. Copyrights and trademarks, you know.

The bookstore is one in my small town where I live, and I have permission to use the description of the place from the owners. I love old bookstores. There's something about the smell of all those words that is intoxicating and special. I've been going to book stores and libraries since I was a kid and fell in love with words, and the smell of anywhere that houses so many books is intoxicating. I will always love it.

It will always smell like home.

Special thanks to all of my readers. This past year has been a great learning process in writing novels, something I've been wanting to do since I was thirteen. I appreciate all the support from all of you who have been loyal readers of my words. Check out my other titles coming soon, and already on sale wherever books are sold online.

Coming soon is a family story of love, redemption, second chances, and heart. Book four is going to be about Arlene's brother Thomas as he struggles to get the farm rolling after setbacks, while falling for a pixie of a gal in Arlene's art dealer friend Meghan.

Book six will follow Arlene Richards, fighting a battle with sobriety, trying to take care of the Richards estate, and meeting a man she used to know in high school that was a bit of a nerdy guy, but has since had a glow up as a horse doctor who is also struggling with sobriety after a failed marriage and a distant, estranged son. For anyone who remembers, Arlene Richards is the wife of Joe, or rather ex-wife. I realized she wasn't such a bad person after all, and I kind of wanted to redeem her after the shit I put her through with the whole Joe and Maxine situation from Book One. Turns out I kind of like her after all. I can empathize with her, since we both face our struggles with addiction in our own ways.

In between these two books will be a novella about the Richards patriarch Thomas, and his wife Catherine. It will be set in 1979 Wilmington NC, and is about two people from different backgrounds coming together after a kiss "puts a fire in her belly that she couldn't ever put out."

The following is a prologue to book 4, I hope you enjoy it.

Thanks again, folks. Love you all, and God bless. Now enjoy this teaser for book 4.

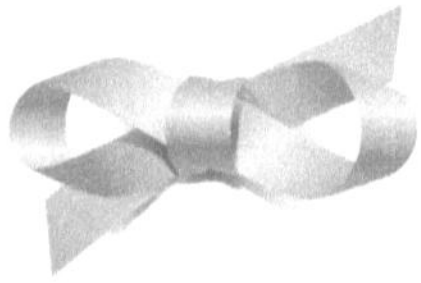

Prologue

Catherine sat in the small Corvette, playing their favorite song, Sugar Sugar. It was their love song. She ran her hand over the white leather driver's seat, wishing he could be there—Thomas, her husband, taken too soon.

The barn was quiet, the stillness only broken by the distant rumble of an approaching afternoon storm. On this day of all days, she thought.

"Mama?" a voice ca

lled from outside the barn. She instantly recognized it as her son, Tommy. A smile touched her lips as a tear slipped down her cheek. She wiped it away. "Mama, you in there?"

"I'm here, baby," she called back.

The barn door slid open behind her, and she turned to see Thomas Richards Jr., all six foot four of him—dark-haired, strong, noble, and handsome. He was the spitting image of his father. If he would just shave that scruffy beard, he'd look like a young Tom Selleck.

"What are you doing out here in the barn again, Ma?" Tommy asked as he approached the white Corvette—a relic from '77. Despite countless offers to buy it, her parents had never been able to part with the car. Too many memories had been made in it.

Thomas Richards Sr. had refused to sell it, not even for a million dollars. The car needed a lot of work—paint had flaked to rust in spots, the oil pan needed replacing, the brake lines had disintegrated, and the interior had become a haven for spiders and insects despite the blue tarp that covered it.

But to Catherine, the car was perfect.

Tommy walked around to the passenger side; his eyes filled with understanding. "Thinking of Dad again, huh?" He bent down and kissed the top of her head, where gray hair mixed with the fading remnants of blonde.

"Yeah, baby," she said softly. "I just miss him." Before he could say anything, she continued, "He would have loved this day. Having you and Arlene and the kids here, and being the Fourth of July too."

"I miss him too, Mama. Everyone does."

Catherine shuddered, looking into the rearview mirror, where memories of dark hazel eyes that she had melted into at a drive-in movie flooded back.

"You gonna be out here much longer?" Tommy asked. "Looks like it's fixing to rain."

"It's okay, baby. I like the rain."

"Don't want you to get sick," he said, glancing at the darkening sky. "Want me to get your umbrella?"

"No," she answered, reaching into the pocket of her blue jeans and pulling out a prescription bottle. "Just give me a minute or two. I'll be in to help Arlene with the hot dogs. Tell Joey and Cathy to wash up for dinner."

"Okay," he said, starting to walk away. "I can still bring you the umbrella if you want."

"No, baby," she said. "I'll be right as rain."

"Okay," he said again. "Love you, Mama."

"Love you too, son."

Tommy walked away, shaking his head. The rain began to lightly patter against the tin roof of the barn. Catherine touched the driver's seat one more time. She opened the prescription bottle, took a tiny white pill, washed it down with a bottle of water she had beside her, and then opened the car door. It creaked, and she made a mental note to come out one day with some WD-40.

Catherine walked to the front of the car. The rain fell more heavily on the tin roof now, and a crack of thunder rumbled in the distance. She sat down on the hood of the Corvette, laid back, and looked up at the high ceiling. She closed her eyes and smiled, feeling the cool drops of rain on her face. She opened her mouth to catch them.

She stayed there for a few minutes, letting the rain soak through her white tee shirt, cooling her skin.

Finally, she sat up, wiped her face, and stood slowly. Pressing her hand against the hood of the car, she whispered, "I miss you so much, baby. It hurts."

She took her hand away and walked slowly toward the sliding barn door. Before leaving, she looked back and smiled at the memory of a rainy night, and the hood of the Corvette that had been a bed to start a family over forty years ago. Then she slid the barn door shut, as the rain slid down her face and helped to hide her tears.